Confessions of a girl in the country

Confessions of a girl in the country

too hot to handle
– sizzling diaries of
desire and discovery

Angelina King

PAVILION

This edition published in the United Kingdom in 2013
First published in the United Kingdom in 2007 by
Pavilion Books
10 Southcombe Street
London W14 0RA

An imprint of Anova Books Company Ltd

Design and layout © Pavilion, 2007, 2013
Text © Pavilion, 2007, 2013
Cover illustration © Jacqueline Bissett, stockillustrations

ISBN 978-1-909108-52-3

A CIP catalogue record for this book is available from the British Library.

10 9 8 7 6 5 4 3 2 1

Reproduction by Rival Colour Ltd, United Kingdom
Printed and bound by 1010 Printing International Ltd, China.

www.anovabooks.com

CONTENTS

PROLOGUE

MONDAY 25TH MAY

I feel like everything is different today. Everything is ruined.

And Henry kissed me goodbye this morning so tenderly! So softly . . .

I even remember noticing it. I mean, I noticed the fact that I noticed it. He always kisses me goodbye in the morning, there's nothing unusual about that, it's just that today, he . . . well, he stroked my hair, and I could feel him watching my face, and when I opened my eyes, he was just studying me, just kind of half smiling. And then he took my face in both his hands and kissed me. Pressed his lips deep into mine. And then he was gone. And I went back to sleep for another ten minutes until the alarm went off again.

And now I'm angry because it's just occurred to me that he was probably feeling guilty and that's why he did that.

Am I so blind? Am I so stupid?

I never thought I'd actually experience that sort of moment. That film moment. No, that's generous. That stupid soap-opera moment when the girl walks in to find her man in bed with someone else. And it's not like I think I'm special. I know that people say, 'It can happen to anyone,' and of course it can, but not to us, not me and

Hen, not us, and if only for the simple reason that I cannot possibly conceive how he could have found the time to pull it off. I mean, except for when we were working, we spent ninety per cent of our lives together. And when we were working, we spent half that time on the phone to each other. We grew up together. We'd known each other for ten years. We lived together! How could this physically happen? I had spoken to him thirty minutes before I caught him. Thirty minutes! Is that all he had needed? Maybe he was with her when I called . . . Oh God, I feel sick.

And to think I thought it would be a treat. My first afternoon off for six months. I'll come back and surprise him . . . what an idiot.

He was at home because he had work to do. So I thought . . . I mean, the way I imagined it, I wasn't even going to distract him from his work, I was just going to lie across his lap and he could stroke my hair as he went through the accounts, or whatever it was he did on that bloody laptop. It wasn't like I was planning to ruin his afternoon, just that I was going to be with him. That's why I didn't tell him. That's why I kept it quiet.

I was going to open the door quietly, creep down the hallway, and find him absorbed in his work, and I'd call out in that funny sitcom voice we did when we first moved in together – 'honey, I'm home' – and he'd look up at me and his cheeks would flush with happiness and he'd smile and say, 'What are you doing here?'

and we'd hug, and eat chocolates and it would all be lovely.

My face is burning as I write this. I want to bury myself in the floorboards.

Some of what I imagined did happen. His cheeks did flush, he did say, 'What are you doing here?' and there was chocolate on the bed, it's just that it was smeared across another girl's breasts. But the worst part of it, the part that makes me want to scream, to put my fist in my mouth and leave it there until I die, is that I did, actually, really, and in an American accent, call out, 'Honey, I'm home.'

I wonder if they laughed when they heard that. I mean, it clearly didn't panic them. They were still in bed when I entered the room. Probably so lost in the moment that they didn't even hear me. Thank God for small mercies, I suppose. But . . .

The whole moment was so surreal, so dreamlike.

The thing I saw first was a bottom. Her bottom.

My hand was on the door, and I saw this bottom, riding on top of a man's hairy legs, and I just kept pushing. And everything slowed down I suppose, because I remember the door opening as if by itself, and I remember thinking, 'Wow, she has an amazing bottom, I wish my bottom were as beautiful as that,' and I remember watching the dimples at the top of the crest and thinking, 'That's probably why this is happening, because of those dimples – how could anyone resist those dimples?' but it hadn't really sunk in why this perfect bottom was riding on top of Henry's hairy legs and so I think I stopped for a moment and just watched them. Watched Henry's face, his eyes locked on hers, the way he seemed so happy, so relaxed, this woman grinding down on him from above and he just kept making circles with his fingers beneath her stomach. It was only later as she was leaving that I noticed all the chocolate that had been on her breasts and front.

And as it dawned on me what I was watching, I became shy. That's the best way that I can describe it. And I am not shy. It's not something I do. I am a trainee barrister. I spend hours in court, addressing people. When it's my turn to speak, people expect me to say something worth listening to, and I make sure it's worth their while. I was called 'Man of the Match' by my boss just last week, over the Senegal trade disposition. I don't do shy. Haven't done it for years. And yet, here I am, my heart thumping through my skin and up to my larynx, blocking it, rendering me speechless.

I can't explain it. What should have been straightforward rage became something else to me. Became embarrassment. Embarrassed that I was there, watching this. Embarrassed that they might see me standing in the doorway and I would have to shout and scream and perform some big dramatic routine. And I had had no chance to prepare this closing. No late-night cramming. This was it. Off the hoof. Improv. Of course

I was upset, of course I was fraught, hurt, volatile, but still, it suddenly felt as if all the pressure of the situation was on me. On my scene. Like I had to make one.

And all I really wanted to do was sneak out again and hope they hadn't noticed me. That way I could come home at a normal time, and curl up with Henry and pretend that none of this ever happened. Because if I did make a scene then all this would have to be dealt with. There would be pain and change and misery and hurt. And I didn't want that. I just wanted things to be as they were.

But then Henry glanced right and caught me straight in the eyes.

'Oh Jesus!' he screamed (actually screamed, in quite a childish way), then threw the poor girl off him and jumped up. The girl let out a 'hey!' before seeing me and suddenly reaching for a towel. And as she rummaged round the room, she smeared this chocolate waste across the sheets, leaving a messy trail that followed her to the end of the bed.

'What are you doing here?' he said, scrambling to cover himself with the sheet and heading towards me.

I went to speak. I went to berate him, to hit her, to attack this situation in the sharp way I deal with most business, but I was defeated. My lungs had no air in them. I let out a little gasp, and tried to swallow more oxygen. It suddenly felt like I was drowning.

The girl with the bottom tried to slink out of the door, but I instinctively put out an arm and stopped her progress. The movement caused her to drop the towel that she was holding in front of her and in the flash of her struggle to catch it again, I saw an image of her chocolate-covered breasts. And God, they were gorgeous, so full and rounded and perky, and I hated that Henry had found this woman, this woman who was more than I was, a woman you would want to cover in chocolate and eat, not hold, not love, but eat, and she mumbled, 'I'm so sorry, I didn't know,' and she crouched under my arm and made her way out of the door.

And Henry was in my face, pleading, mumbling, a string of words all running together, 'It wasn't I didn't know you were coming back I'm sorry it was a mistake I love you please calm down please please . . .'

I remember lashing out at him, just flailing my arms in an undignified way, landing small slaps on his bare chest and he tried to grab my wrists and I think I screamed, 'Get off me!' and then I turned to hear the girl leave the flat and I thought, my God, it's just the two of us again, alone in our home, like it always is, and I was so overwhelmed by it all that I thought, don't say anything, let him deal with it, you keep your mouth shut and . . .

And I guess I was screaming because Henry was trying to hold me, and when I pushed him away and put my hands to my face, they came away wet, and it was obvious that I was crying, that I had been crying, and that I had no idea how long I had been crying for.

WEDNESDAY 27TH MAY

Gerry came to meet me for a coffee today in Mayfair. He was worried about me. I hadn't told him everything. I mean, he knew that Henry had gone to stay with Matt and that we were breaking up, but he didn't know why. I hadn't given him all the details. It's no one's business, after all.

'I never trusted him,' was the first thing he said to me.

'What do you mean? Why didn't you say anything?'

I think Henry had actually called him, which pisses me off. Called my brother to apologize! Is that sick? I think that's sick.

Anyway, it was nice to see Gerry. I think I had been pretending I was OK for too long. But I guess that's what family does. Makes you realize you aren't OK. They see straight through the front.

And now Gerry was telling me things I never knew. Making me feel more stupid than I already did.

'It's just . . . I remember when I was fourteen or something, and he came round for our family Sunday Christmas thing, and he kept sneaking outside to smoke cigarettes and I just thought . . . Well, I went to join him for one and he started asking me about girls and stuff, you know, trying to be all big brother and everything, and when I told him about Jenny, he was like, 'how old is she?' and 'she sounds nice' and all that kind of thing. And then he started giving me advice and I was thinking . . . well, you know what I mean.'

I love how my brother can get so far with a subject and then he just cuts himself off, like he is worried he might be boring you. The way to deal with him is to give him a gentle nudge.

'No, I don't know what you mean. Wasn't he just trying to bond with you?'

He picked up the conversation as if it had never paused.

'Well, yes, I mean, I know he was, it's just that, he started giving me advice and I thought, "You're in love with my sister. You shouldn't be telling me this stuff."'

'What did he tell you?'

'Just stuff.'

'What kind of stuff?'

'I don't know, boys stuff, that kind of stuff.'

'Gerry, I don't know what kind of stuff.'

I took a sip from my coffee and stared into it. Gerry doesn't like eye contact when he gets to the point of his story. It makes him uncomfortable.

'He said . . .' and then he took a deep breath like it was all too much for him. The next words came out from his mouth like a waterfall.

'He said, "Tell her you want to touch her and then when you get her alone, hold her up against the wall, not violently, but firmly, and stick your tongue in her mouth and squeeze her breasts and then . . ."'

'What?' I pushed.

'Then . . . then you hold her down and you can do whatever you want to her. Because, if you have got that far, you know she's yours.'

I had to swallow my coffee hard to make sure I didn't spit it out.

'He said that!'

'Well, yeah, and I just thought, "I don't know what you're trying to do here, but I'm fourteen years old. I don't want to hear this stuff. From my sister's boyfriend. I don't want to think that that's what you're doing with her." I mean was it?'

'No! Of course not! He was always very gentle with me!'

'Then why did he say that?'

'I don't know. I'm shocked.'

'I'm just saying . . .'

'Why did you never tell me this?'

'Because you loved him.'

'But . . .'

I felt a sudden pang for my brother. He was younger than me, and he always seemed young. Even now, at twenty-two, he was like this sensitive boy that didn't quite fit into the hustle and bustle of the real world. I had the overwhelming urge to apologize to him. Like he had been violated.

'I'm sorry you felt like that. I'm sorry he said that to you.'

'It's not your fault.'

'No, I know, I'm just sorry you didn't feel you could talk to me about that. That must have been hard.'

'Well, it didn't really happen again. I just hated that feeling.'

'Uh-huh.'

'Like I was betraying you. Just by listening to him. Just by smiling along while he said those things. Pretending like I was learning something from him.'

He stirred his coffee again. Then drifted off.

'And then you were together for eight more years. And I just had to hope I was wrong about him.'

And it was weird because I suddenly felt very defensive, like Gerry was saying my whole life had been a sham.

'He was just trying to bond with you, Gerry. He didn't . . . he never treated me badly. He was good to me.'

Gerry looked up, surprised by the sudden U-turn in my attitude. Then he laughed.

'Yup. Yup. He was definitely good to you.'

'Don't be like that, Gerry.'

'I'm just saying . . .'

'Well, don't! Please . . .'

I was losing this connection with my brother. Like we were on a phone call that suddenly lost its signal.

I know he had come to see me to be sweet. I just didn't know what I wanted. From anyone.

I needed something to hold on to. I put my hand on Gerry's arm. He looked at it. Gerry doesn't like to be touched. I pulled it away.

At work, no one seems to notice a change in me. Which is good. I don't want their attention. I haven't told anyone. And I only cry in the cubicles. That's it. No one sees me. No one knows.

Henry called me about six o'clock. He wanted to talk. I told him to go away and that I wasn't ready to talk to him. I shouldn't have even answered the phone. Because when I hung up, all I wanted to do was cry again. And I had already cried too much.

SUNDAY 31ST MAY

I have nothing to write today. I am so depressed. I just want to lie in bed all day and hold my duvet over my face. What am I supposed to do? Everything is gone. Henry is not here. My friends say things that basically mean, 'I told you so'. And my family seem disappointed in me. Why did this happen?

Maybe it's just Sunday. My first Sunday alone. For a long, long time.

I hate Henry for making me feel like this. We're supposed to meet on Tuesday for drinks. 'To discuss things . . .' I don't want to see him. I think

I'll want to be with him if I see him. I think I'll want to forgive him.

I don't even want to watch TV. I just want to cry. How am I capable of producing so many tears?

I am lost.

I need to change my life.

MONDAY 1ST JUNE

I feel better today. It is good to be working. Nice to take your mind off things. I took all the minutes of the meetings today. Usually I let Ann do it, but I wanted to be completely engaged in the case. And it worked. I didn't think about Henry once.

Genevieve emailed me back. Says I should go and stay with her for the week. That might be nice. A week in the country. Get away from it all.

I should probably cancel my drinks with Henry.

TUESDAY 2ND JUNE

I saw Henry for drinks. Of course I did.

He met me in Balan's in Soho. Why he wanted to meet there, I have no idea, but when I arrived he was sitting in a corner booth. He stood up to greet me with a big smile. I didn't smile back. He tried to kiss me, and his lips fell on my cheek as I turned my head. His hug was short-lived and awkward.

I put down my handbag and took a seat. The music was quite loud, which I was pleased about because it drowned out the sound of my thumping heart. I know I must have looked angry, but the truth was I was speechless, and my hands were shaking.

It was like when I had discovered them in my bed. I didn't know what I was supposed to do. Was I supposed to slap him? Say something clever? I felt lost by the whole situation. And seeing him, feeling him next to me, Henry, my Henry, my rock, I don't . . . I just didn't know what to do.

So I sat looking away from him and let him stumble through it. You have the right to remain silent.

'I'm glad you came to meet me. I was worried you wouldn't.'

'I nearly didn't.'

'That's fair enough. I'm glad you did, though.'

Silence.

The waiter came over. Poured the water and looked at us. He frowned. He could taste the atmosphere.

'Can we get a bottle of house red?' Henry asked and the waiter nodded, and I rolled my eyes.

'You're not going to get me drunk.'

'I'm not trying to. I just thought . . . this is quite difficult . . . for both of us . . . and a glass of wine might make it more pleasant.'

'You fucked someone in our bed. It can't be pleasant.'

And my ears suddenly burned, and my skin prickled, because the words had just come out and they were hot and right and tears punched at my eyeballs, but not because I was sad, but because I had said something I hadn't said for over a week. And it shocked Henry too. Which made me feel good.

'I'm sorry.'

'Why did you do it?'

'I don't know.'

'Yes you do.'

He rubbed his forehead furiously, like it was a magic eight ball, and it would suddenly reveal the answer.

'Because I'm a man.'

Anything you say, can and will be used against you in a court of law.

'Brilliant,' I said, and wanted to punch something, but instead I locked my eyes with his and asked, 'Because you're a man?'

'And we need things and you're not . . .' He trailed off, embarrassed.

'What?' I asked, suddenly scared to hear the answer.

'Nothing. I love you. You know that. I've always loved you. I didn't want to hurt you.'

'Then why did you do it?'

'Because . . . Because I need to sometimes.'

'What do you mean, "sometimes"?'

'This wasn't the first time. You must have realized that.'

I don't want to remember this moment, because it was so awful, but I know that if I were ever asked to describe how I felt when he said that, I would say that it felt like cold metal was swilling round my mouth.

I didn't say much. When the wine came, I drank it quickly. He kept talking softly. At one point he tried to grab my hand and I moved it away, and squeezed it in my lap.

'We were always together. And it was always great. And you make me laugh, and you make me happy, and you care about me and you care for me, but . . . it's not . . . I don't want to sound ungrateful . . . It's not – God this sounds awful – it's the sex. You're not . . .'

He looked up and I was still staring at him. I think this is what they call rock bottom. I couldn't feel any more of this pain and shame and anger, it had peaked, so I just let him continue.

'The sex is good. It's nice. It's loving. I want to say I love you every time we have sex, you know?' He smiled and sighed, then continued. 'But it's not . . . It's not enough. And I'm sorry. Because that's the truth. And I think, I think I've tried to change things with you, I've tried to make it happen, but you are not open. You're not. You're just not. And there's nothing I can do about that. So I found it elsewhere. Because I love you. I didn't want to lose you. I just had to do what I had to do.'

I cradled my glass. Contemplated where to put its contents. In my mouth or across his face?

'And you had to fuck other women?' I said in my most controlled voice.

'Yes. I suppose. I had to find what I couldn't find with you.'

'I didn't satisfy you?'

'No, you did. Completely. Emotionally at least.'

The conversation couldn't have got any worse.

'Do you not find me attractive?'

'Of course I do. You're just not . . . open.'

'You never asked me to be.'

'I tried. I did try.'

'When?'

'I don't know off the top of my head.'

'Well, think!' I said, and I know that my voice did flicker a notch and I wished it hadn't.

'OK, OK. When you caught me looking at porn on the computer. Remember? You told me to turn it off –'

'Of course I did! You were my boyfriend!'

'You wouldn't even look!'

'What? What are you even talking about?'

'I'm just saying if you'd been –'

'What, if I'd been a magic girlfriend, I would have said, "Oh, that's great, you're wanking in our bedroom over pictures of other girls"!'

'See, you don't even get it, you can't even conceive that –'

'How are you making this into my fault?'

'It's not your fault, per se, it's just –'

'Per se!'

'Look, you're not making this easy for me, I'm trying to explain something to you.'

'I'm so sorry I'm not helping out here . . . just . . . make it clear.'

He ran his fingers through his hair. Took a deep drink from his glass. He leaned forward on the table.

'You don't seem to need what I need. Sexually. It just isn't . . . a . . . component of your make-up . . . you just like to be held, and that's it. I . . . need more.'

I stood up. I hadn't planned to, but my legs had clearly decided for me. I let out a small 'fuck you' and walked away. And when I got into the bracing air of the street, I decided to walk all the way home.

I passed drunks, and couples, and bikes, and buses, and I let the wind push the tears back with my hair.

It took me an hour but when I got there, I knew. Fuck you, Henry. I'm going to change my life. I'm going to accept Genevieve's offer. Disappear for a week. And you are going to miss me so much.

CHAPTER ONE

I am writing this on the train. I already feel better. As the carriage moves further and further away from the city, I feel like I'm shedding some skin. Like I am getting lighter. It will be lovely to see Genevieve. We haven't spent time together, well, properly, for about five years.

I'm looking out the windows. The landscape has already begun to change. From tower blocks and concrete and lampposts, to patches of green to big acres of yellow, the sun shining down on them as if the whole earth is being cleansed around me.

I miss the country, actually. I forget what it is like to have space around you. To feel real nature under your feet. The way the earth is malleable. The way you can smell it and feel it change. And the smell seems alive. You only realize the sickly chemical tang of London when you are away from it.

Genevieve seems to be doing well. I have missed her. It's nice that we've kept up this email relationship, but we used to be best friends. At boarding school, she was . . . well, I guess she was the one who seemed ahead of the crowd, a little bit older than all of us. Where I was ashamed of and embarrassed by my changing body, she would not hesitate to show me her emerging breasts, wandering topless around the room we shared as soon as she got in from classes. At the end of term disco, she was the one who made the first move across the dance floor when the rest of us stood against the walls, girls on one side, boys on the other, like a giant game of British Bulldog. And she was the one who would sneak back in late at night with stories of boys and what they had done and how they had looked and where they had touched her.

She was this whirlwind of exploration and energy, and because my life always seemed so difficult and nervous, I used to long to be around her, just because I knew I would have to be more exciting to earn the right to be in her presence.

Once, when she had stayed with my parents for a weekend, she had snuck out while I was asleep. I don't remember who she was trying to meet, but I know my mum caught her and sat her down at the kitchen table to talk. And when I crept downstairs to listen, Genevieve was crying and mum later told me that she thought she was wild because her father was dead and she didn't have any discipline in her life. But Genevieve never talked about that.

I remember when I first stayed with Genevieve. I was fifteen. I went down to her mother's estate for a week in half term . . .

God, I'd forgotten that incident! It has just come back to me so vividly. I think the man opposite me is wondering why I blushed!

It was before Henry . . .

It was about halfway through the holidays. Genevieve's mother had gone away to Argentina again and we were being 'looked after' by the help. And 'the help', this poor beleaguered woman called Sharon who lived in the small cottage at the end of the garden, had already given up trying to keep an eye on us.

Genevieve said she was going to 'show me something'. I didn't like to get into trouble like she did, but I followed her anyway (what else was I going to do?) and so we ran through the fields, over the fence and down to the neighbours' estate.

I've forgotten the name of the neighbours, actually. Something very important-sounding like Jenkins-Booth or something like that. The estate took up sixty acres, including stables that housed about seven beautiful black horses.

The horses were grazing and swishing their tails in the sun. I remember I was slightly out of breath and Genevieve grabbed my arm and told me to 'shhh' and suddenly we were crawling towards the side of these huge stables. And she checked her watch and giggled. 'What?' I asked. 'Shhh,' she shot back.

She interlinked her fingers in mine (I remember it so clearly, her soft, small, lithe little fingers!) and pulled me quietly up to the wall of the stable. She sat up on her knees, then put her head up to the wall, closed one eye and peeked through a very small hole that had corroded through the wood. She beamed.

Then, not looking back at me, she gestured for me to come forward.

And when I think about it, it's funny how innocent I was, because I think I thought I was going to see a beautiful horse or something like that, since Genevieve had always loved horses. Like she was going to show me a unicorn or something magical. But when I looked through the hole, the stables were empty. All the horses were out in the paddock.

Across the barn, though, facing the corner of the room, with hay stuck to the soles of his shoes, was a boy, slightly older than us. His trousers were hanging round his ankles and his calf muscles were tensed so tight, they looked like they might rip out from under his skin. As my eyes travelled up I saw the cleave of his buttocks, just dipping under the threads of his shirt. And his arm was moving vigorously in front of him, his elbow moving up and down like a piston on an engine.

I did not know what I was seeing. That's embarrassing! How naïve was I? I mean, I had had sex explained to me, I knew how everything worked, but this! There was no woman there! Was he unwell? What was he doing?

And why did I instinctively feel, in the pit of my stomach, that I wanted to kiss this boy?

Genevieve abruptly snorted a big laugh, then quickly slapped her own mouth shut with her hand. But it was too late. The boy turned around, and as he turned, I became rooted to the spot by the sight of his cock. It was so firm and hard and it seemed to rear up when it saw us, and he was gripping it so tightly in his hand that it looked like a sword that he might try to attack us with.

The boy grabbed his trousers and roughly pulled them up. 'Oi!' he shouted and made to run out from the stables.

'Run!' called Genevieve, and she grabbed me and we both scrambled for the side of the fence, and I felt my heart beating in my ears, because we were being chased and I felt frightened and I didn't want to look behind me because I knew he was close and I didn't want him to see my face.

That's very vivid, that thought, actually. I didn't want him to see my face. Because I thought he might hate me.

'Oi, you bitches! Come here!' he shouted, and Genevieve tripped on some shrubs and for a moment I was going to keep running, but I couldn't leave her, and not because I wasn't a coward, but because I didn't want him to think I was a coward. I turned back for her only to see the boy pounce on her and hold her down, and Genevieve was giggling and I thought, 'How can you laugh? How can you laugh when you are clearly in mortal danger?' and I froze on the spot.

The boy lifted her up and she continued to giggle, and he brought her back down, her arms flailing in a small act of struggle, and then he laid her across his knee.

And there was a pause, while he held her down with one strong forearm and searched behind him with his other. What was it he was looking for? Genevieve's long hair bounced up and down as she tried to raise her head up to see what he was doing. And then there was a look of quiet triumph in his eyes.

With a tearing sound, he pulled out a thick clump of bracken from the ground. And I thought, now is the time I have to do something, now is the time I have to scream, to get help, to stop him hurting her – but I did nothing. I just stood there, my knees slightly floaty, watching.

Genevieve finally stopped laughing and she looked across at me with a quizzical look, but I couldn't take my eyes off the branch. There was the sound of wind whipping through the bracken. And then, thwack! He brought the branch down with such force that I, and not Genevieve, let out a gasp. I felt tears prick my eyes with the injustice of it all, and here I was just watching, too scared to stop it. Thwack! Again the branch struck her, and – thwack! – it came down again and – thwack! – poor Genevieve, the pain she must be feeling, but – thwack! – why wasn't she screaming?

When I glanced down at Genevieve's face, I saw something I didn't expect. Her eyes were closed and she had a smile on her face I had never seen before. It was a smile I can now describe as satisfaction.

And then the boy looked at me. Stared me straight in the eyes, his arm raised high over Genevieve. And I held his gaze. Would not let him stare me down, although I know he wanted to. Not taking his eyes off me – thwack! – he brought the branch down one last time.

He groaned a little then rolled off his knees on to his back.

Genevieve sniffed and made to get up. She smoothed out her skirt and came towards me. The boy leaned up on his elbows and looked at me again. 'You want it?' he asked. I shook my head and realized my tongue was pressed against my lips.

'Then clear off, the pair of you.' Genevieve and I stumbled away, not talking, me stunned into silence and her rubbing away at her bottom.

When we got into her room, she pulled down her pants and showed me her raw cheeks. 'Isn't he amazing?' she said.

How funny . . . what a strange girl. I can't believe she's got her own practice now! I guess you have to be a little bit crazy to be a therapist. It takes one to know one, and all that.

I wonder if she looks different.

The train is pulling in. I will report back later.

CHAPTER TWO

LATER

What a lovely day! My God, Genevieve is amazing. She has such a wonderful energy. I feel better than I have felt in weeks. Better than I've felt since . . . Do you know what, I haven't even thought about Henry for the last few hours, and I refuse to right now.

I got a taxi from the station and drove with the windows down through the country lanes up to Genevieve's house. The air was so refreshing; it blew through my hair and sprinkled my face with dew. The driver kept looking at me and smiling.

'You look happy,' he said.

And I just smiled. I felt free, I guess. I was away from my life. Different surroundings, different people, no work worries, no nothing. Just going to see an old friend.

The car pulled up the drive and, although it was still splendid, peppered with an array of gorgeous flowers, I felt like the fences were closer to the sides of the car than they used to be.

I was a child when I was last here! A young girl! The place seemed so enormous, so luxurious when I was small. And now . . . it was manageable. Not overbearing. A girl could live here and be happy. No wonder Gen's emails were always so chirpy.

As the car drove away, and I wheeled my suitcase towards the huge oak door, I heard a scream of delight.

'SOPHIE!'

Out from the side of the house, dropping a watering can, came Genevieve, her arms outstretched. She was wearing a lovely white silk dressing gown that was loosely tied, exposing her gorgeous midriff. She hugged me tight, and I suddenly burst into tears.

'Oh, darling!' cried Genevieve, and as quickly as I started, my tears sealed up again, and I was laughing, and I buried my face in her hair, still long, still perfectly straight, and we laughed, hugged and spun on the spot.

Within moments, she had given me a gown and the two of us sat on sun loungers at the top of the garden, where the view extends down the hill to the vast acres ahead. The sun glinted off the spikes of grass, little diamonds of light on crystal glass.

Genevieve poured me another glass of sangria from a decanter.

'God, I feel like I'm in Spain or something,' I said, and she laughed and raised her glass: 'Senorita . . .'

After we had got through the you-look-so-greats (and she does), and the it's-been-too-longs (and it has), we settled into a more thoughtful conversation.

And what she told me next really shocked me.

I had asked her how the practice was going. I hadn't realized that she conducted all her business from her own home.

'Well, it's private and it means people can explore themselves or each other in a safe place,' she said.

'What do you mean?' I asked.

'You know what I do . . .' she said, that old mischievous look in her eye.

'Well, yes, you're a therapist,' I replied.

'What kind of therapist am I?'

I stared at her. Why was she testing me? I knew what she did.

'You're a kind of life coach, I suppose. For psychological problems.' She kept staring at me. 'Aren't you?'

'I'm a sex therapist.'

I laughed inadvertently.

'Of sorts . . .'

She was serious.

'Are you?' I asked, trying to look equally serious.

'What else could I do?' she said and laughed.

And then she explained it to me.

'I help people to find their inner sexuality. Not what they have been programmed to be, not what they think they should be. Not even what they think they want to be. I try to free them from themselves. All the years. The nature versus nurture. All these psychological barriers we pick up from birth. Strip them away and what you are left with is the most sexually fulfilled person there is. And if you are satisfied sexually, then the rest of your life takes care of itself.'

I think that was how she described it. I found it all quite astonishing.

'Are there a lot of other therapists like you?'

'There's no one like me,' she said, and then laughed again. 'There are, of course, many sex therapists, it's just that I have developed my own style.'

'And what's that?' I asked.

'A lot more experimentation. Challenge yourself. Let things happen. That sort of thing.'

She looked at me, her eyes taking on a devilish twinkle.

'You'd be surprised what you can get away with in the country.'

Always. Her life was always more exciting than mine. I shouldn't have let our friendship slip away. Then I wouldn't be twenty-six years old and suddenly feel like a child again.

'How come you never told me about this?' I asked, feeling slightly wounded by this news that I had not been privy to.

'Sweetheart,' she said, in a way that only Genevieve could pull off, 'You haven't been to stay for five years. I kept you up to date with most things. But this . . . the reason my practice is a success around here, is because it is private. Completely private. The only people who come here are recommended by previous clients. That's it. No one else. So I didn't want to send you emails about it because I didn't want anyone at your work or wherever finding out about it.'

'I wouldn't have told anyone if you had asked me not to!' I said defensively.

'Sophie, I don't think you would have. The point is, you're here now. And I'm excited you are. Because now I can tell you everything. And if I didn't trust you, I wouldn't have invited you here.'

And then she said something that sent a little shiver up my spine.

'And the best part is, when you called me, I thought . . . I could help you.'

She leaned back on her lounger. She took a long drink from her glass. I watched her. Tried to read her eyes as they stared off into the view ahead. Nothing.

Part of me had wanted to argue with her, to defend myself, to say, 'How dare you, I don't need your help, I'm fine, I'm successful, I'm perfect,' but I couldn't ignore the small flame that seemed to have started up inside me, a feeling I guess like adrenaline, when she had said those words, 'I could help you'.

So I lay back too. Closed my eyes. Felt the sun pour itself across my body. She could help me, I thought. What have I got to lose?

I started to talk. About Henry, about how we began, about how we finished, about the whole sorry incident in our bed.

Genevieve is, I can say without any doubt, a good therapist! I told her everything!

She has that natural way about her, something in her eyes, in her face, that makes you want to spill your guts and you know that she'll love you for it, and not judge you, and sympathize, and take some of that weight for you, and God, it felt good to get it off my chest.

And when I finished the whole sorry debacle, she asked me about what dreams I had been having . . .

I told her about the one I had before I left. It started like the other dreams. There I was walking down the street towards mine and Henry's flat, with my stomach clenching as I got nearer the door. And, as in the other dreams, I walked into the flat and called out, and got no answer and walked to our bedroom. But as I got nearer the door, this is where the dream became different. This time the gnawing I had felt inside me turned to a feeling of expectation, to a feeling of excitement.

And as the door to the bedroom opened, instead of Henry and the girl ignoring me, they turned to face me and, with a soft look in her eyes, the girl beckoned me towards them. She did not move from straddling Henry. Her firm thighs stayed locked on top of his, but as I approached the bed, she reached out her hand and put it to my face.

'Kiss him,' she said, and she had a kind of Russian accent, which was very odd, because in real life she had had a Chelsea accent.

And I felt nervous to kiss Henry, like when we had very first kissed, but I was nervous because she would be watching. But she guided my head down towards Henry's and Henry raised his head off the pillow and our lips connected, and it was such a soft kiss, such a loving kiss, and just as I was becoming fully absorbed in it, I felt something behind me.

The girl had placed her mouth on my back, on the area of skin between my neck and shoulders. She began to press down on it with her teeth, pulling small mounds of flesh inside her mouth.

Henry began to probe my mouth with his tongue, sliding it inside, exploring my tongue with his and taking deep breaths in through his nose. He placed his hand over my thigh. Lifted up the skirt I was wearing. Then took hold of a handful of my tights, and ripped them right off me.

I gasped as the cotton fell away, but he stopped me from crying out by putting his tongue back in my mouth. And I felt my insides begin to tingle, as he brought his hand closer to my vagina and I waited for him to touch it.

He used two fingers to spread my lips, parted them like the soft skin of a fruit, and then he delved roughly inside, his fingers heading straight past the mouth and into the darkness.

Then I felt fingers on my breasts, and the girl had managed to remove my bra and was tickling my nipples, holding them between two fingers, and squeezing them as she continued to ride Henry and bite into my neck.

As she pushed further into him, and pinched one of my breasts, I became so overwhelmed by it all that I closed my eyes because there seemed to be a kind of sensory overload to the whole thing. When I opened my eyes again, I was awake and bathed in a sheen of sweat.

When I told Genevieve this she smiled.

'That's kind of sick, isn't it?' I asked her, embarrassed that I had just made this confession.

'Not at all,' she answered promptly. 'What's sick? You wanted to be included. That's what happened. In all your other dreams, in the actual reality of that moment, you were left outside of all this pleasure that was taking place in your own bed. And you wanted to be included.'

'I find that hard to believe. I wanted to kill them! I didn't want pleasure.'

'But your subconscious doesn't listen to your head voice. That's why our dreams reveal truths. You wanted to be included.'

I sat back and ruminated on this. Was she right? Was I sorry to have been left out? It seemed ridiculous. But that dream . . .

Later that day, we picked vegetables from a little plot at the bottom of the hill. It was so satisfying to plunge my hands into the mud and tear carrots out of the earth, right from the root, to hear the satisfying 'ccrrrrk!' as it came free. And we talked and laughed and it felt so refreshing to work for our dinner, to actually 'work' for it, and then we were in her gorgeous kitchen, chopping and slicing and steaming and cooking on the Aga. Over dinner we finished off a wonderful bottle of red wine, and then leaned back, stuffed, satisfied and content.

Genevieve made some fresh coffee, and we sat out on the patio, the air just cool enough to require a jumper, but still very pleasant. I looked up at the sky and was amazed by the thousands of stars I could see. 'Gen!' I exclaimed, 'It's beautiful.'

'You forget about the stars in the city, don't you?'

'We just don't get them in the city,' I laughed.

We sat watching them, perhaps waiting for one of them to shoot across the sky.

Genevieve spoke.

'You know what I would ask you if you were a client?'

'What would you ask me?'

'I'd ask you if when you woke up from that dream you masturbated.'

I nearly spit out my mouthful of coffee.

'Genevieve!'

'It's a legitimate question, Sophie. You had a sexual dream. And when most people wake from an erotic fantasy, they like to conclude it.'

'But Sophie! That was my boyfriend with another woman!'

'It doesn't matter the who's and why's. The point is that within the dream you were aroused.'

I didn't say anything. I was struggling to not shut her out, which is what my instinct was telling me to do. And then sweetly she said, 'I'm not trying to upset you, Sophie. I'm only talking here.'

I took a deep breath and answered her.

'I'm not like you, Genevieve. You know that. I'm not so . . .' I couldn't find the words. 'You know what Henry told me when we met up again. He told me that I wasn't "open". Sexually. And I was so upset about this, and so confused, but then the more I thought about it, I thought, well, he's probably right. And you asking me that, just makes me feel . . . I don't know.'

I did know. I wanted to say. Pathetic. Unfeminine. Abnormal.

'How was your sex life with Henry?' she asked.

'Oh, it was fine. It was lovely. He was always very gentle. Very loving.'

'Did he make you come?'

I was glad it was dark out there so she couldn't see me blush.

'Um, yes, yes, I think so –'

'You think so!' laughed Genevieve.

I told her not to laugh and she apologized. 'It's just . . . I think you would know if you reached orgasm with him.'

'Well, I mean . . .' I didn't quite know how to explain it. 'It's like . . . it was always so nice to have him inside me . . . like he was filling me up, like we were becoming connected. And it would feel . . .' I cannot tell you how hard I found it to talk about this. But I persevered. If this holiday was going to be for anything, it was going to make me face my fears.

'It feels like we are going up a hill, like we're running, and I get very excited that we are going up this hill, and we run and we run, but . . . I never get to the top of the hill. I know that there's something over the other side. I know it would be nice to roll all the way down to the bottom on the other side, but with Henry . . . I could never quite see over the brow of the hill. But. You know. The hill was really, really nice anyway.'

Then I laughed, embarrassed. 'I must sound like such a prude.'

'Not at all, Sophie. That's all quite normal, I think. What about when you're alone?'

I sighed. I knew she wouldn't like this answer.

'I haven't masturbated in eight years. I didn't think I should. I had Henry.'

I could tell Sophie was shocked. I could tell she wanted to shout and scream and tell me I was crazy, but thankfully she just paused, sighed, and then inhaled.

'Do you think you've had an orgasm before?' she asked softly.

'I don't know,' I said, and felt very tearful again, like I had just admitted a shameful secret.

Because I did feel ashamed. All these magazines I see in the office, about women having orgasms at work and at home and everywhere and I always felt like, what's the big deal? I am in love with Henry. He cares about me and takes care of me and we laugh together and if I were to ask for anything more, then that would just seem greedy.

'Well, this is fantastic,' Genevieve said.

'Why on earth is this fantastic?' I asked.

'Because you've got all this wonderful stuff to discover. I'm almost jealous!'

CHAPTER THREE

So, in a way I am supposed to chart what happened next. When Genevieve heard I kept a diary, she encouraged me to write up all this stuff. She said it would help my 'sexual development' if I could refer back to the things I liked. Or not.

She said it was time to explore my body. She gave me a list of three things to do.

1. Stand in front of the mirror. Naked. Look at your body. Explore it with your hands. Focus on what you like. Do not focus on the negative. Every part of you is beautiful when put in the right perspective.
2. Run a bath. Think of a scene that you find sexually exciting. Real or imaginary. Play the scene over in your mind. Focus on the parts of it that you find particularly exciting. If it is just one image, freeze that image in your mind.
3. Get in the bath. Explore your body while concentrating on the scene. Take your time. Touch yourself. Find the rhythm that suits you. Let go of the tension. Allow it to happen.

I sat on my bed looking at the list. I was glad that my room was so far from Genevieve's. Far enough that

I could be sure she couldn't hear anything. I felt strangely self-conscious, as if I was being videotaped. I wondered if I could do anything on the list, but at least the thought of a hot bath seemed like a good idea.

I dimmed the lights. The room now reflected my mental state: dreamy, spacious and tingling with a kind of electric static from all the day's revelations. The bed is large with creamy white sheets and when you lie on it, you feel as if you might get swallowed up. There is a small window in a diamond shape that looks over the garden. You can see nothing but trees and stars and twinkling windows from the village in the distance. The walls are white, but are crisscrossed by large wooden beams. The floor has a deep plush carpet that feels heavenly beneath your bare feet, the strands sprouting up between your toes.

I realized that I hadn't looked at my body in much detail before. Not since puberty, I guess. I spend a lot of time on my face and hair. A lot of time. In fact, most mornings I get up a full hour before I need to leave for work. That gives me twenty minutes to shower and shave my legs. Then ten minutes to moisturize my legs and my face. Then another twenty for hair and make-up. With the ten minutes left over I grab a cup of coffee, some porridge and then head out the door.

But for all that time I spend staring at my face – analyzing the structure of my cheekbones, the way my eyes look puffy for the first twenty minutes of the day and the way my mouth is surprisingly red without lipstick, in comparison to my paler skin tone – I have never really studied my body.

I know my body is OK. It's not fat, I have reasonable-sized breasts and they don't sag, and I know that Henry always appreciated them, but that's about it. It's my body. It's what I use to put clothes on and carry around my head! I think if I were to think positively about myself, I would always concentrate on my face. After all, that's what people read when they meet you, isn't it?

I faced the full-length mirror that lay against the wall and began to peel off my clothes, one at a time. It felt odd doing this, watching myself. I felt almost embarrassed every time I watched my own hands, the way they were so delicate, as if they were taking this more seriously than I was.

I wriggled my bum and my skirt fell to my ankles. I stepped out of it and looked at my legs standing inside the white panties. They were nice legs, I suppose. Surprisingly toned. I leaned over and ran my hand from the tip of my foot, sliding it over the tender muscle of my calf, over the firm ridge of my thigh. I guess walking to work had paid off. They were nice to touch. All that moisturizing had been a good idea.

I raised myself up again. My hands were near my buttocks. I shut my eyes for a moment. Inhaled. My panties fell to the floor. I turned my back to the mirror. I was still wearing my bra. I turned my head over my shoulder and looked at myself from behind.

My bum. I slid my hand over it, let a finger slide between the two buttocks and squeezed softly.

It was a nice bum, actually. Curvy and firm. I squeezed it again, and the self-conscious feeling turned into something else. Something more exciting. A tingling in my loins.

I reached up and unclipped my bra. I let the straps roll down my arms. One clip hung between my fingers and I let it go. I put my hands on both breasts, holding them firmly. Then I turned to face the mirror.

My nipples were quite beautiful when they were erect. Sort of the right size, I suppose. Fresh-looking, with tiny spikes around the edges, like glints in the iris of an eye. I ran my fingers across them, then let them hang. And they stayed fairly pert. Alert, even. They seemed soft and proud all at once. I smiled to myself. This was ridiculous! I was turning myself on . . .

I let my eyes glance down to my vagina. And there it was. The clean thin strip of hair, that I had kept like that since I was eighteen, and the small folds peeking out from underneath.

Hang on a second. Wasn't I supposed to run a bath? Wasn't I supposed to focus on something?

I stopped staring at myself and opened the door to the en suite bathroom. The bath had small candles around it, and a box of matches. I hurriedly lit them and turned on the huge taps at the end of the bath. The pipes chugged and whirred and stuttered until finally a wide stream of hot water began to pump out. I put the plug in and picked up a bottle of aromatherapy oils that sat by the bath in a plush little basket.

I unscrewed the top and let a long line of oil fall into the bath. The aroma was lavender and patchouli, and the bottle read 'Sensual Essence'.

Leaving the door open, I went back into the bedroom. The steam from the bath wafted into the room. There was a wicker chair by the cupboard with two big pillows on it, one for sitting on and one for leaning against. I pulled the chair in front of the mirror and sat in it. I looked at myself.

There was a feeling growing in my pussy. Like it needed to be touched. Or rubbed. Like the sweet ecstasy of a mosquito bite that you wait to scratch, and hold off on, and then when you finally rub your hand over it, it sends waves of satisfaction all over you.

I reached down to my pussy. Let my fingers glide through the tight line of pubic hair. Over the crest of my clitoris. Through the middle of my two lips. My pussy was slick now, moist. This was how it used to feel when I was at school.

Terrified of being caught. Touching myself under the duvet, alone in the dorm. Desperately watching the door, ready to stop if someone came in.

I spread my lips slightly and looked in the mirror. It was so strange. To see something that has been a part of you for your whole life. And to feel like now is the first time you are really seeing it.

And it was beautiful.

So beautiful that I wanted to touch it, to feel it from the outside, and the inside and let it know that I wouldn't neglect it again. I felt the need to enter it with my finger, to explore it.

I eased a finger inside and let it circle around. As it pressed up, I let out a little gasp. On the inside, as if I were beckoning someone who was outside with my finger, I felt a small ridge. And stroking that ridge sent little spasms of pleasure deep inside me.

I moved further inside, my eyes automatically closing. The canal of my pussy was warm and wet, and I allowed another finger to follow. Up ahead my finger came across a small sort of nub that seemed to extend from somewhere high above and point down into my pussy. I touched it.

And my whole body jerked.

Oh my God! What had I found here?

I slid my finger across it again.

Oh my God . . .

What I had discovered was an untapped zone of pleasure, deep within me. I ran my fingers up and down and over this nub, and my stomach muscles contracted and my hair caught on the wicker but I couldn't stop pressing it and circling it and I thought, can this be it, is this the answer, oh God! Why does this feel so good!

Oh Jesus! What about climbing the hill and the edge and the feeling of not seeing over the top and oh . . . my . . . God . . .

My body wrenched and tensed and spasmed and I brought a hand up to my breasts, tried to hold them both in one hand, as if they might fly away from me if I didn't squeeze them; and with my other hand I held on to my pussy and I felt tears coming to my eyes, because it had been so long, because it had been so easy, so ridiculously good, and because it felt so fucking right . . .

My heart was thumping blood around my body and everything felt so engorged, so flooded with endorphins.

And as I tried to get my breath back, I laughed. What a waste! Eight years and I could have been doing this! Eight years of looking out for other things, working on my self-esteem and trying to prove myself through my career, and all that time I could have been doing this!

And then all I thought was . . .

. . . get me in that bath!

The bath was so hot that it burned my skin, but I held on to the edges and waited for the burn to pass and leave my skin tingling. The oil reflected on the water and the light from the candles increased the misty quality of the air. I dipped my head under for a moment, rose back up, then ran my hand through my hair, forcing the drips of water out.

I lay my head against the back of the tub and stretched out my legs, so my feet were either side of the taps.

I felt so hungry, so ready to go again. Partly because I wanted the pleasure and partly because I wanted to prove to myself that it wasn't a fluke. Some kind of random explosion caused by the drink and the air and the change in my surroundings.

I wanted to know that I could control the pleasure. That I could make myself feel that good.

I looked down at my body as it lay in the tub. My nipples were poking in and out of the water and my legs were glistening. I raised them higher and slid both hands back to my pussy. I rested my right hand over the mound, let it cup it, pressing down slightly so as to send the hot water in a pulse towards my pussy.

I had forgotten number two on the list. The fantasy.

What did I need to think of to turn me on? What was my thing?

I shut my eyes and the first thing I saw, as I had done repeatedly, was the scene from my life, and my dream: interrupting Henry with the girl.

I opened my eyes again. There was no way I was going to pleasure myself to images of my own betrayal! But as I closed my eyes again, I couldn't help going back to it.

The image of her bottom over his thighs, the way he raised his head up, surrendering to her body.

I wanted to change the image. I needed to.

What if that was me, I thought? What if I was on top of him?

I ran a finger over the fold that covered my clitoris. Because of the oil it slid straight under it and pressed the button of my clit. I opened my eyes again. Was this so wrong? To fantasize about a man who had hurt me so much? Is this what I really wanted? To be with Henry again?

I closed my eyes, and pressed three fingers together over my clitoris. I began to circle them anticlockwise, and went back to my image.

But it had changed.

I was on the bottom looking up. Henry was on top. He was smiling as he leaned back, penetrating me.

Although the physical sensation was good, the image didn't seem right. It was disconnected. I tried again, moving my hand slightly faster.

Now I was on my front and Henry was taking me from behind. My face was pressed sideways into the pillow and he kept pushing into me in a slow gentle rhythm. And now I couldn't see him, so I guess that was better, but it still felt wrong. I brought my other hand to my face, and realized I was frowning heavily.

I opened my eyes again. Maybe I had overstretched myself. Maybe another orgasm was too much to ask. One step at a time maybe. One step at a time.

I brought my hands back to the side of the tub, and exhaled heavily. It had been a long day. Maybe just sleep on it.

The water was still hot, so I didn't want to get out just yet. Just one more minute, I kept telling myself. The smell from the candles was starting to infuse me again. I readjusted myself, placed a towel behind my head and closed my eyes.

What was it I had liked in the dream? What was it that had turned me on, I kept asking myself.

I kept trying to replay the scene as I had seen it in the dream. Henry kisses me, yes, I remember that, but then there is something happening behind me, something going on at the same time, oh yes, the girl! The girl, biting me, pressing her teeth into my shoulder. And when I thought about it, it wasn't the fact that she was a girl, it was the contrast that turned me on.

The fact that while Henry was being gentle with me, she was being hard. While he was caressing me with his lips, she was using her teeth. While he stroked my buttocks, she pinched my nipples.

And as I focused on that feeling, I probed inside myself again, my finger stretching out for the nub, the orb of pleasure, and this time I used my other hand to circle my clitoris, and as it did, and as the water began to vibrate as my muscles contracted, I tried to focus on one image, to pick one bit to play over and over again and I found it.

Lips on my lips, teeth on my shoulder. Fingers on my pussy, nails on my tits. Tongue in my mouth, hair on my neck. Covered by flesh. In the middle of flesh. Surrounded by flesh. Suffocated by flesh.

I pressed harder against my clitoris and kept the rhythm steady, my other fingers dancing around the nub and my calf muscles tensed so hard that I thought I might get cramp, and I know I was squeezing my eyes shut, but I wanted it so bad, I could feel it, I needed it, and this time I was aware of the hill, I was climbing it again, but there was the top, I could see the top, and then . . .

Two different rushes surged through my body. Like an explosion. And I think I screamed. I don't know what happened. All I know is that five minutes later I was still catching my breath and there was water on the floor.

And here I am finishing this entry. Ready for bed. Excited to curl up in my sheets.

And feel them against my supple skin.

What will tomorrow hold?

CHAPTER FOUR

TUESDAY 9TH JUNE

I slept like a baby last night.

Genevieve didn't wake me, and with no alarm I slept through to eleven. That means I slept for ten hours, which is the longest I have slept in about a year. I really think there is something to this whole country air thing.

I slipped into my dressing gown and tiptoed downstairs. Strangely, I felt a real thrill of excitement, the fact that I was going to share with Genevieve what had transpired in the night. Like a kid wanting to impress a parent. Look how well I did!

When I got to the kitchen she wasn't there, but the cafetière was full, and I could hear murmuring down the corridor. I realized she must be having a session. I looked up and stared towards the 'work' corridor.

It was tempting . . . but I was hungry. So I ate.

The coffee slipped inside me and fired up all my synapses. I was awake and alive and I stepped outside into the fresh air and took a deep, full gulp of it. It was beautiful. And for a moment, I thought about work and about Henry and about London, and I thought, who needs it? I'm here now. And it's wondrous.

Back in the kitchen I sat down at the table, munching my toast and leafing through Genevieve's health magazines. This herb is good for this, that herb is good for that. Everything seemed so complicated . . .

Now I know Genevieve had made a big deal about the whole privacy issue of her business yesterday, and I know, as a lawyer, I completely and totally understand and respect that, and I know that had someone asked me if I would ever behave in this way, I would have resolutely said, 'No! How dare you even think that of me!' But . . .

How often are you in the middle of nowhere, at a sex therapist's practice, hearing male groans coming from behind a door?

My only justification for my actions is that perhaps I thought I might never be in this situation ever again, and it would be crazy not to at least learn something from the experience.

At the side of the kitchen was a door connecting to a narrow passageway. The passageway was lit by small windows, but the walls were a different hue from the rest of the house, making it clear the distinction between the Practice and the House. I padded softly down the corridor.

I carried two mugs of coffee with me. My reasoning was that if anyone came out and caught me, I could say I was just coming to see if anyone wanted a coffee. Since when did I become so devious?

As I got close to the end of the passageway, I could hear the man groaning in short sharp breaths and whispering something, quite quickly, that I couldn't quite make out. Thankfully the passageway was carpeted, so my bare feet made little sound.

The door to the 'office', or 'recreation room' or whatever Genevieve likes to call it, is a big wooden one, with black metal fasteners on the side of it. But it seems that the door is slightly bigger than the frame for it, and so I think the edge of the door has been shaved off at a slight angle to accommodate it.

And what this means, is that if you line yourself up against the walls, you can see a slither of light coming through the door. And if you position yourself correctly, as I indeed did, you can see a piece of what is going on inside.

I held my breath and brought the two cups of coffee up to my chest to try to control any movement or shaking. I peeked inside. What I could make out was a man's hand over his penis. The penis was lying back across his stomach and he was grabbing it and rubbing it. But he wasn't rubbing it in a vigorous way; it was almost idle, like he was petting it, or stroking it, but not even in a particularly sexual way; just pulling it about as a pre-sexual child might.

The penis was only half-erect so it kind of lulled and stood up and fell down.

Although I could only make out his mid-section, the man was clearly quite old, perhaps in his sixties, given the wrinkly nature of his hand and the grey tufts of pubic hair. He was obviously lying on a sort of ottoman, his feet hanging off the end.

I could hear Genevieve, her voice a constant soft mantra. Where was she? I would have to guess that she was on the left-hand side, perhaps facing the man from a distance. Was she sitting? Standing? I couldn't tell. The man was mumbling and I breathed out softly, then took a deep breath in and tried to tune into their words.

Genevieve kept repeating something: 'der der der der like this' or something. And then the man would say, 'No, I don't think so' and then there would be a rustling and Genevieve would repeat her words. I squinted, as if that would make the phrase become clearer.

The man pulled harder on his penis, and this time it grew firmer.

I knew I should leave immediately, just return to the kitchen and forget I ever saw anything, but for some reason my feet were firmly planted to the floor. I could leave now, I thought. But if I do, I'll never know exactly what it is Genevieve keeps repeating. And since I've come this far . . .

I leaned my head back and tried to focus. It was so odd. This man, this old man, touching himself, in front of another woman. There was something so relaxed about the energy in the room. Something not tense. I guess, when I thought about it, it seemed strangely unsexual. Being that open. Just lying there playing with himself.

Somehow, I mused, this is not what I consider sexual.

Sexual to me, it seems, is something clandestine, hidden, tense and possibly even shameful. I smiled at this revelation. I'm really screwed up, I thought.

And then suddenly Genevieve stepped into the frame and I jumped a little. Her slender body momentarily blocked the light and I could see she was wearing her silk gown. She kneeled down at the side of the man with her back to me.

'Does der der der der like this?' she whispered. He began to mumble faster. I felt my heart thumping in my ears. I tried to control my breathing.

Then I understood what it was she was saying: 'Does it mean you can't like this?'

Then she did something, but I couldn't tell what, something with her arms stretched out in front of her, and I could see the belt of her gown was hanging by the floor, which must have meant it was open, and the man groaned louder, 'No it doesn't.'

She asked him the question again and he groaned louder still, and there was the sound of friction, something rubbing, faster and faster, and his groans went on increasing and just when she asked him the question again, a voice spoke from behind me and I jumped and spilled all the coffee on my bare feet, and yelped and dropped the mugs.

The voice had said, 'Naughty girl.'

In my panic, I saw that Genevieve glanced behind her, then back, and cooed softly to the old man, 'It's just the birds, keep going . . .' and I was crouched on the floor, wiping my feet and I was shhhhing myself.

Who had said that? Whose voice was it? It was a strong voice with a deep timbre. I looked along the passageway and could see the outline of a male figure.

The physique was clearly broad, that of someone who had grown up lifting things, big shoulders and a wide chest. The man was silhouetted, but I could see that he held a finger to his lips.

I crouched down holding the mugs and, trying to ignore the scorching feeling on my feet, crept back along the corridor, slightly afraid that this man was security or something I didn't know about, and worried that I must be in big trouble.

He was leaning against the doorframe, one leg crossed over the other at the ankle, and his arms were folded. His hair was thick and slightly scruffy, with a side parting that had sort of lost its place. His thick mouth was fixed in a kind of smirk.

And his eyes . . . his eyes were deep. Black.

And when I looked in them, there was some kind of electricity that passed between us. A strange, chemical sort of feeling that I hadn't experienced for some time . . .

He said nothing, just stared at me, and I looked back at him like a little girl who had been caught stealing. I whispered, 'I'm a friend of Genevieve's, I'm staying with her, I just wanted to see if they wanted any coffee.'

The man turned and moved into the kitchen. I followed and closed the door behind me. With his back to me, he said, 'Right . . .'

I tried to compose myself, but blurted out, 'I burned my feet.' Why did I say that?

He turned back to me. 'Sit down,' he said, pulling out one of the wooden chairs. I put the mugs down and sat on the chair.

The man, clearly comfortable within this house, moved over to the taps and grabbed the washing-up bowl from the sink. He filled it with cold water then came over to me. He kneeled down at my feet and reached out for them.

And it was so surreal. The way I instinctively let this big man, this stranger, put his wide hands on my ankles. He gripped them firmly and I could feel the skin of his palms against my shins. His skin was hard, firm, taut. Worker's hands, my mother would have said.

I kept my eyes on my legs. They looked like daisy stalks in his palms. He placed my feet in the water and I felt a shock of cold, an almost audible 'sssss', come off my skin. I winced but didn't want him to know that it hurt, so recomposed my face into a deadpan.

He reached up and picked a tea towel off the table, then dipped it in the water and lifted out one of my feet. He squeezed the towel out over my foot, and the cold water dripped off my skin and splashed back into the bowl, sending bubbles over my other foot.

And this was repeated with the other foot. But here's the thing that was most surreal . . .

We weren't talking to each other.

A man, who had just caught me eavesdropping on a private sex session was washing my feet, and I was letting him, and we were doing it in silence. He wouldn't even look up at me. He just stayed focused on my feet.

A good few moments passed, and my feet began to feel numb. I dared to speak.

'Thank you. I just . . . I was checking on them.'

'You were spying on them,' he said, still not acknowledging my face.

'I wasn't . . . I mean . . .' I was speechless. A sudden flash of reality hit me, and I felt a spark of my business self as my career mind kicked in. Who was this man? Who was he to make judgments of me?

'What are you doing here?' I said, emboldened by a new sense of self-righteousness. 'For all I know, you could be a burglar.'

He laughed, a small, not entirely truthful laugh, and looked up at me with those eyes. I found it difficult to hold his gaze this time, and shamefully looked away.

'I'm not a burglar,' he said. 'I was dropping something off for Genevieve.'

'Oh,' I replied.

'Is that all right with you?' he asked, a new tone of bitterness in his voice.

He then stood up rather abruptly. 'You'll be fine,' he said, as my feet splashed back into the bowl.

At that moment, Genevieve walked in and I jumped again like I had been caught for the second time that day. She stood in the doorway and looked at me, my feet soaked in water, the man pacing around by the sink, and she sighed. I assumed she was angry and tried to find the right words to placate her, but she spoke first in her sensual way.

'Naughty girl.'

'That's what I said,' piped up the man.

'I'm so sorry, Genevieve, I was looking for something, I mean, I meant to bring you a coffee . . .'

She cut me off with a laugh. 'It's OK. I think you got away with it. We still managed to finish the session.'

I knew I was blushing and I looked down. Genevieve strode across the room towards the man and kissed him firmly on the cheek.

For some reason, I was rooted to the chair, which only made me feel more like a child, out of place now in this kitchen that minutes ago had felt so comfortable.

'Genevieve, I . . .' I tried again, but she moved over to the kettle and switched it on, saying, 'I see you two have reacquainted yourselves.'

What? I thought. Reacquainted?

'Yeah,' said the man. 'I was trying to spare your friend any embarrassment.'

'I burned my feet,' I piped up, then blushed again.

Why did I keep saying that?

The man smirked again. 'Yeah. She dropped the coffee. That she was bringing for you.'

Genevieve laughed. 'Oh, sweetheart. Are you all right?'

'I'm fine,' I said, in what I knew was a distinctly sulky tone, my career mind having once again left the building.

The man drank a full glass of water in one, and then made for the door. He turned back to say, 'I left your package by the door.'

'Oh, thank you, see you later,' she called, and the man gave a perfunctory glance back to me and left, crashing out the door.

'Bye,' I murmured.

Genevieve watched him walk away out of the window and sighed a little. She turned back to me.

'So . . .'

I was still a little stunned by everything.

'So what?'

'So how was it last night?'

'Oh –' and suddenly all those thrilling feelings I had felt, and the desire to tell her everything had gone, and all I felt was lost again.

Genevieve bounded over to the table and took a seat.

'How weird for you to see Samuel? It must have been a decade since you saw him?' Samuel?

I apologized and told Genevieve I didn't know who Samuel was.

'Don't be ridiculous,' she laughed. 'We used to watch him every day. The stableboy. You remember?'

And with that, my whole face filled with blood, and my hair stood on end, because that's what I had felt when the man had looked at me in the passageway, that feeling, that moment when he had stared at me, his arm raised up as he held down little Genevieve!

'Oh my God!' I said. 'The stableboy! I'd forgotten all about him.'

'You know, he owns the manor now. Inherited it. The whole place is his.'

'That's incredible.'

'I know. Doesn't know what to do with it. Never married again. Just lives there alone with a few staff. Quite sad, really. Still loves to ride, though.'

'When was he married?'

'Oh, a while ago . . .'

And then Genevieve outlined a large part of Samuel's biography, how he had been an orphan, how his aunt and uncle had set him to work with the horses, how he had married a girl called Lyndsay, and how they had seemed quite happy until she died in a car accident on her way back from London. And since then Samuel, apparently, lives in his stately home, still working with the horses and generally keeping himself to himself.

It was like something out of a Bronte novel.

'I can't believe that's him. I mean, I don't really remember him that well.'

'We used to watch him every day!' insisted Genevieve.

'Once,' I countered.

'Don't lie! It was every day. And by the end of the week it was you demanding that we go and watch!'

I knew that wasn't true – was it? – and told her so.

'Well, fine, whatever,' she replied, and set about cleaning up the water that was covering the floor.

I stepped outside and inhaled deeply. Trying to regain myself. So that I could give Genevieve my report.

I sat for a moment and looked across the vista.

I told Genevieve about the previous night and she was, as usual, lovely about it and thrilled and excited for me, and she told me how I had progressed at lightning speed and that I should be applauded. I felt so excited when she said that, but the feeling was immediately countered by the question I then asked myself: Why do you need all this validation? What about just being pleased with yourself?

And then I thought about it. If Genevieve was going to 'help' me, if she was actually going to use her skills, then in the interest of full disclosure, I should vocalize that thought. Which I did. And she once again applauded me, telling me that awareness was the next step on the road to enlightenment.

'Sexually?' I asked.

'Everythingly,' she smiled.

Tonight Genevieve will take me out for Phase Two of my 'mission'.

We spent the afternoon talking about objectives. I was still slightly reluctant to treat my visit as 'official therapy' so had refused her offer of sitting in her 'recreation office', instead keeping our dialogues to the kitchen table.

She asked me more questions about my sexual development, which brought up a few interesting things, like the fact that I learned most things from her at school. And here we were again in the circle of life! 'Hakuna matata,' she said and we both laughed.

She told me the next step in my development was to go out of my comfort zone. Since Henry had been my only lover, she asked me to go over the history a bit. She asked me to tell her the story of how Henry and I had met. Although she knew it, she wanted me to tell her the details that came up in my mind.

Henry had gone to the boys' school that was twinned with ours. I was a keen swimmer at school, and was allowed out in the early evenings to go to the town's swimming baths.

One evening I was doing several lengths, and through my goggles I was aware of someone watching me from the side of the pool. I tried to block the thought from my mind. There were lots of people there, and the boy could have just been taking a rest. But you know that feeling you have like you are being watched? That's what I felt that day.

Like he was only watching me.

I continued my lengths, but I realized that I was going faster, even though I was on the final phase of exhaustion. I was going faster for a reason. I wanted him to be impressed. I was showing off.

Every time my head popped up for a breath, I realized that I was favouring my right side, instead of the more professional way of favouring both. My swimming coach would have been furious! But I was doing it so that I could catch a glimpse of the boy watching me.

And there he sat, a towel wrapped around his waist, his arms folded across his chest, his head still, but his eyes definitely tracing my journey.

On my final length I began to slow down and feel butterflies in my stomach. Because if I were to finish now, that would mean that I had to get out. And see him. And maybe he would want to talk to me. And I wouldn't know what to say.

So when I had finished, I got out sheepishly at the far side of the pool from him, grabbed my towel and headed straight for the changing rooms.

I remember how nervous I was in that shower. Nervous that he might be waiting for me outside. And nervous that he might not be.

It's strange reliving that feeling. It was so . . . exciting.

When I came out of the baths and started walking

back towards school, he was there, sitting by the bus stop. I instinctively looked down. He stood up.

As I passed him, he said something. I can't remember what he said exactly, but what I do remember is that as soon as he spoke, his voice quivered and for the first time, I realized that he must be nervous too. And as soon as I understood that, I relaxed a bit.

I let him walk me back to school and we pretended to talk about different swimming strokes and how he had admired my style. And then, by the bushes at the gates, we said goodbye, and he asked if he could take me to the cinema on Saturday. I remember pausing and saying, 'Er . . . yeah, if you want.' I even remember thinking Genevieve would have been proud of me for saying that. For being so cool with him!

Genevieve smiled at that bit. 'I'd forgotten that,' she said. 'That's sweet.'

Then she asked me another personal question.

'Do you remember if you thought about him sexually that night? Did you masturbate to thoughts of him?'

The answer was no. The truth was I didn't think of him sexually, really. And then it hit me hard. Henry was a boy then. And I guess I'd always seen him as that. I mean, yes, we had grown up together and lived together and had sex together, but somewhere, deep in my mind, he was always that thin-armed boy who had been so nervous at the bus stop.

'And that's not sexy, is it?' asked Genevieve.

'But I loved him so deeply,' I said, my eyes glazing at the thought.

'That's not what I asked,' said Genevieve.

She asked me about my first sexual encounter with him, and my mind immediately jumped to when we had held hands for the first time. Held hands! I thought. That's how unsexual it was!

We were in the cinema. God, I wish I could remember the film, but all the way through it I was aware of his hand on the divider between the seats, just sitting there, the hand ever so slowly creeping across the arm of the chair. And I kept my hand firmly on my thigh.

And eventually, I think literally an hour into the movie, his little finger reached out and touched mine, really softly, as if I wouldn't notice, and then slowly his other fingers followed suit, until finally, eventually, our hands were entwined.

There was a tingle inside me at that moment. I remember that.

'What kind of a tingle?' asked Genevieve.

'What do you mean?' I said.

'Well . . . was it the kind of tingle you had last night. In the bath?'

'No.'

And I felt bad for a moment, like I had betrayed something in the past.

'That tingle was love, Genevieve.'

Genevieve blinked slowly and smiled back at me.

'And that's wonderful,' she said. 'Many people would kill for that kind of tingle.'

She paused. 'But we're here to explore the other tingle. The tingle you didn't get with Henry.'

'OK,' I said, and inhaled, ready for my next instructions.

Tonight we are to go to a pub. It is a nice pub, so I'm told. There are many friendly people there and, on this particular night, there is always a kind of party. I am to find someone in this pub and kiss them. It doesn't matter who. It has to be my choice. And I have to do this, because Genevieve says that I have never gone after something sexually.

In my sex life, I have always been the one who has been chased, the one who has been taken.

Tonight, I am to take someone.

Leave my comfort zone.

Do something I've never done before.

'And after all,' Genevieve told me after my multiple protests, 'it's only a kiss. . .'

CHAPTER FIVE

LATER

Wow. What an evening! Unbelievable. I'm exhilarated and embarrassed and giggly and confused and elated! What was I thinking?

I completed my mission! I did exactly as I was told. Well . . . plus a bit extra . . .

We arrived at this pub and, well, I don't know what I was expecting, but it was like a small festival, not a dingy old-man-type place. There were chairs out on the lawn and candles and a bonfire and inside the walls were decked out with flowers and plants and the whole place felt like something out of *A Midsummer Night's Dream.*

There were jugglers and people singing and dancing and it was so freeing, so alive. There wasn't that slightly dangerous feel you have in the city, just people outside enjoying themselves.

Genevieve and I had chosen our outfits together, just like in the old days. She wore a flowing white skirt and a tight-fitting top, and I was in a soft, summery dress. I had bought it last summer but never really had the chance to wear it as I ended up working so late most nights. It felt good to be in soft, flowing cotton. The breeze was glazing the air with a pleasant temperate warmth.

Genevieve was the perfect 'date', ushering me inside and then outside by the hand, and introducing me to all the friendly faces. Normally, I find meeting numerous people a bore – it's something I connect with work and with making 'contacts' – but tonight was different for one reason.

Each new person could be a conquest.

Each new face could be the one I kissed.

Each handshake could lead to something else.

Suddenly the world was alive with possibilities.

There was very much a community feel to the place. Everyone seemed to know something about everyone else, there were lots of questions for Genevieve, and she seemed to have told a lot of people about me.

'So you're the girl!' exclaimed a portly woman who was watching over a barbecue. 'Genevieve has been so excited about you coming to stay! Are you having a wonderful time?' She smiled.

'It's lovely,' I said, and she inhaled the air deeply.

'Makes a nice change, doesn't it? Oliver and I moved here twenty years ago. Never looked back.'

'I don't blame you,' I laughed and bit into the hot dog that she served me. Ketchup burst over the sides of the bun and I sidestepped it, letting it splatter on the grass. It was delicious.

We drank cider and talked and laughed and watched the bonfire and joined a circle of people singing songs, but I didn't know any of the words, so I just watched Genevieve and laughed at her tunelessness.

Children ran around and played leapfrog and screamed and giggled and it all seemed so pure to me. Families, summer, green, full moon, beauty.

So pure, in fact, that I momentarily forgot my mission, and began to enjoy the simple joys of people having a good time. But at about ten o'clock, I went to the bar to get us some more drinks. I was feeling slightly woozy from all the cider, and a little bit dreamy.

The barmaid, Lisa, who I had been introduced to at the start of the evening, took my order. She leaned in close and I was suddenly aware of her fabulous cleavage. I had not initially noticed it, because her blouse had been laced up more tightly earlier.

Lisa handed me the drinks and leaned towards me. She beckoned with her finger, so I brought my ear close to her lips. They brushed softly against my skin as they spoke.

'You're beautiful. You know that?'

I felt the hairs on my neck bristle and my skin turn a little red.

'Thank you,' I replied.

I kept my face near hers, unsure of whether to pull away. Her fringe tickled the top of my ear lobe.

'That'll be four pounds, please,' she said, and I quickly stood upright and pulled out some cash. I think I blustered something like 'thank you so much for the drinks' and then she held my hand for a moment as I passed her the money.

'See you later,' she said, and was gone to the till.

I returned to Genevieve who was sitting on a large, cushioned garden swing. I handed her a tankard and sat down next to her. The swing rocked quite suddenly and we both spilled a little of our drinks and laughed and steadied ourselves.

I felt such a love for Genevieve at that moment. Such a warmth to be back with someone I had once been so attached to. And here we were again, on this beautiful night, like children, giggling and sat on a swing.

'So what about you,' I asked, because I felt like most of this week had been solely about me.

'What about me?' she asked in her coquettish way, and I smiled and said something like, 'A man . . . men, relationships. What about all that stuff?'

She sighed and sipped her drink and said, 'It's never been about that for me, Sophie. I don't believe in "the one" or the thing that happens, or all that stuff. Life is too polymorphous; it's too exciting to settle for "one thing". I mean, imagine' – and at this point she took my hand – 'imagine what my life would be like if I had settled for one man. I'm pretty sure he wouldn't let me continue my practice. I'm pretty sure I couldn't be here now, on a whim, with you. There's just so much to experience. I can't . . . I mean, I can't not live my life . . .'

As I listened to her, in spite of the pleasantness of the evening, I couldn't help but wonder if I completely believed her. I mean, it's all well and good being open to new experiences and all that, but being closed to a bond you can have with another human being, that deep connection that comes from sharing your life, was that not something to aspire to?

I tried to address this cautiously. 'You experience all these people, and that's all amazing, but have you ever . . . tried a long-term relationship?'

'Of course I have,' she laughed. 'But we were both too curious. In the end we couldn't satisfy each other completely so we returned to our lives.'

'Who was he?' I asked.

'Samuel,' she answered.

'The stableboy!' I spluttered.

'The stableman,' she corrected and smiled.

'What happened?' I asked, and she looked towards the bonfire for a minute.

'Neither of us were so good at intimacy, that was all.'

'I'm sorry,' I said, and I wish I hadn't, because it sounded patronizing and clumsy.

'Don't be sorry,' she said, and at that she kissed my nose. 'I don't think I'm like everyone else. I don't want to share everything with someone. I want to share it with everyone. I don't think I'm missing anything.'

'But,' I continued, unable to let it go, 'there's just something that you can't experience, something about history with a person, some kind of connection that goes beyond the surface . . .'

'Like you had with Henry.'

Her words stung me hard in my abdomen and I regretted ever beginning this conversation. I looked away for a moment and tried to catch my breath. Genevieve snuggled up to me and put her head on my chest.

'I have a deep connection with someone. I have history. I have a feeling of closeness that has never left over the years. Do you know who I have that with? You.'

And we hugged and let the swing sway us for a bit.

'Don't you have something you need to do before the night is over?' said Genevieve mysteriously.

'Yes, yes,' I said, 'I got distracted.'

There was a man in the pub's garden who looked slightly out of place. He wore a suit, where no one else did, and held his gait very stiffly. He stood near the barbecue observing everything and talking quietly to the occasional person. I had noticed him earlier and was surprised Genevieve hadn't introduced me to him, as I had met most of the other people there.

I looked over at him again and he was still stiffly sipping his drink and gazing out at a group of people coming to the dregs of their evening, some curled up in big woolly jumpers, some sat in the corners of the pub, drunk and exhausted.

I asked Genevieve, 'Who is that man?'

'Why did you pick him?' she laughed.

'I didn't pick him. I just wondered who he was.'

'Lord Keatley.'

'Is he married?'

'Yes, many times.'

I laughed, and asked why he looked so miserable.

'He's not miserable – he's a voyeur.'

'Oh, I see,' I said, thinking, what? 'Is he one of your clients?'

'He was,' she whispered.

'Did you cure him?'

Genevieve turned to me.

'Maybe. He's still a voyeur. But at least now he's comfortable with it.' She giggled and made her way over to him.

I felt very self-conscious all of a sudden, like I was being set up, or judged. There was no one near me, so I just sat there with my left arm cupping my right.

Genevieve arrived at the man. He stayed fairly upright and, as the firelight caught his face, I could see he had quite an attractive face. Rugged, slightly Roman, with thick lips. His greying hair was full and slickly coiffured.

My friend whispered something in his ear, and his face turned towards me. I became aware of my posture, and remembered back to one of my legal lessons, about exuding confidence. I immediately let my arms slide down to my sides, pulled my shoulders gently back, and let my breasts push forward in my dress. I kept my eyeline somewhere in the distance, but made sure that he could see my eyes sparkle in the moonlight.

Thinking back on this moment, it's funny how I was so ready to be assessed, to be judged.

I glanced back over at them. Genevieve had her arm around him and, somehow, she seemed to have cracked his glacial stance. He was crouched slightly now, whispering and smiling in her ear. Without looking, he pointed his hand towards me, and I knew they were talking about me.

Maybe this was it. Maybe my mission was now officially in gear. I was to kiss the Lord of the Manor! A kiss . . .

I could now feel the cold in the breeze. Perhaps I was nervous, perhaps the reality of the situation had finally hit me. Did I want to kiss a stranger? It seemed so . . . so unlike me.

But what was it Genevieve had told me on the first day: challenge yourself.

And now Genevieve was making her way back towards me. Alone.

Maybe I had failed the test somehow. I didn't know. Maybe she had told him about my mission. But wasn't the point of the mission to get me to do the 'chasing', get me to be the aggressor?

I felt angry at Genevieve for a moment, like she might have humiliated me. But when she came over, she said, 'He wants you to come on Friday.'

'Come to what?'

'I was hoping he'd ask.'

'What is it?' I persisted.

And then she smiled. 'It will be your final task. A party. A real party.'

She smiled again and, nudging me, said, 'If you want to complete tonight's mission with him, it would be a good challenge.'

'But, but what did you say to him? Did you say I wanted to kiss him or something?'

'No,' she reassured me. 'I told him you were my best friend and had come to stay. That was all. He said you were beautiful. And he invited you to his party.'

OK. I finished my drink. So.

'What am I doing again?' I laughed.

'Your mission is to kiss someone. That's all. Go.'

My heart rate was accelerating as I approached the man. He remained standing by the side of the pub. He made no approach, just held his ground. What was I going to say to him?

I had asked Genevieve and she had told me not to plan anything. Just see what happened in 'the moment'. At this point, as my feet pressed closer along the grass towards him, I thought that was the worst advice ever!

So, you're a friend of Genevieve's? Or . . . Isn't it beautiful out here? Or . . . Do you come here often?

I now had empathy for men everywhere, all these people I had assumed were cocky suits trying to talk to me after work. I had never thought about how hard it is to start a conversation with a stranger.

But maybe there shouldn't be a conversation. Maybe I should just kiss him? Maybe that was all I needed to do. A conversation might be misleading. All I needed was the kiss.

I was now only metres away from him. And still he made no move. Just stood there, watching me approach. I stepped forward. I could hear him inhale, ready to accept whatever it was I was about to do. Help me out here, I willed from behind my eyes, but he stayed motionless.

As I passed the open door to the pub, I could feel the change in temperature, the warmth that escaped into the colder air outside. I felt the breeze tickle my legs. I was moments away from him. Let go, I heard Genevieve's voice say in my head, let it happen.

At which point I ducked inside the pub, away from the man and headed straight for the toilet.

I wasn't ready for this. This wasn't me. Just wandering up to a stranger and kissing him. I mean, it all sounded exciting and great, but really, it's something the Genevieves of this world do, not the Sophies.

I held my wrist under the cold tap and let the icy water sprinkle my fast-beating pulse, cooling my insides. I stared at my reflection. My cheeks were red, warm. My hair had feathered a little in the humidity. I looked like someone who had been in bed all day. Warm and tired.

The door to the toilets opened.

'Hello, you,' a voice said, and I looked up. It was Lisa the barmaid. She smiled at me, the sweetest smile I had received all night.

'Hello,' I said, turning off the tap.

Lisa stepped in front of the mirror and began to wash her hands.

'Just got to get rid of this lemon juice. It's all over my fingers.'

She was standing so close to me that I could feel her thigh against mine.

I looked at her reflection in the mirror.

'So, is Genevieve giving you missions?' she asked, not looking up.

'You know about them?' I asked, glad to be connecting with her.

'She gave me missions a while ago.'

'Did they work?'

And then she looked up at me.

'What do you think?' she purred.

I don't know what came over me. I reached up to her face, took her cheeks between both my hands and turned it to me. She stopped the tap. And then, very gently, looked into my eyes, her lashes floating up like butterflies.

Very, very slowly, I brought her face towards mine. I looked down at her lips; thick and red, the colour of ripe cherries. As she came closer, her eyes closed, and at that point so did mine.

Our lips pressed together. Connected. I'd never touched lips that soft. Lips without stubble. Lips without cracks. Just soft, sensuous lips. She pressed hard against my mouth, and then let the pressure off again, and I could feel her breath brush across my cheek, and I realized that I had been holding my breath, and so I let it out, and then . . .

Then she opened her lips, moved them slightly apart, and so I followed, keeping our lips locked and, without thinking about it, instinctively, my tongue edged forward and met with hers, two slick muscles sliding over each other. Her tongue was sweet and delicious and it came into my mouth, sliding behind my top lip and exploring further into the crevices beyond.

Our lips closed again and then reopened, and this time my tongue went far into her mouth, playfully wrestling with hers, our lips bunched together, forming a ring, and I was inside her mouth and it tasted of apples and sunflower oil and sweetness, just a sweetness I had never experienced before.

A moment passed, and I seemed to suddenly be aware of myself again. Like I had floated back inside my body. I let go of her face and stepped back a moment. Her eyes remained closed and she murmured a small 'mmmmm'.

I looked at that mouth and thought, just a little more . . .

My insides were tingling and firing sparks.

I leaned forward again and let my lips fall back on to hers, let her saliva spill into mine, our tongues dancing a slow dance of exploration, a dance of life. And this time, my hands began to move over her back, to hold her tighter to me, and she responded, and then I was aware of those breasts of hers pressing against mine, just as our lips were, just as our tongues were.

My hands wandered down her back and grazed her bottom, slid past it and continued down to the backs of her legs. They then returned to a spot they had enjoyed, the curve between her buttocks and her legs, that deep, defined perfect curve.

She placed a hand on my thigh and ran a finger slowly up my leg. Our kissing became more passionate and I could feel my legs start to shake slightly. I wanted to lie down. I wanted to roll on top of her.

Her tongue was now more passionate, more alive, probing deeper and deeper into my mouth, and I wondered how that would feel down there, if I were brave enough, if I would dare, then the door to the ladies' opened, and we abruptly stopped, and both turned on taps and pretended to wash our hands.

I felt so flushed and hot, I was worried that my dampness might show through my dress. It was Mrs Hemborough. She held the door and stared at us, as we sniffed and laughed.

'Right,' she commented. 'I see . . . Don't mind me.'

And I burst out laughing, I felt so intoxicated, and so did Lisa, and then Mrs Hemborough said, 'Shall I just close up the bar?' and Lisa smiled and said, 'That sounds like a good idea.'

And we both laughed and Mrs Hemborough closed the door behind her.

We stared at each other through the mirror. Lisa was leaning forward on her elbows, pushing her breasts out over her top.

The interruption had put a burst of reality into the room. What was I doing? I suppose I had completed my mission. I had been the aggressor. The conqueror. I had looked at something and I had taken it. And yet . . . and yet . . .

It was a woman. I had not known I could feel so excited in this way with a woman before. It felt odd. And naughty. And right.

And then I reflected on something else. Lisa had been sympathetic to my 'mission', she had understood and perhaps helped me out. But if I was really going to do this properly, if I was really going to challenge myself and find out what I didn't even know I liked, I needed to go one step further.

Which is the intellectual version of events that my brain came up with to disguise the fact that I was tingling between my legs and I didn't want to stop.

I turned to Lisa and pushed open a door to a toilet. The cubicle was clean but small. There was only a little legroom, so I stood with my back flat against the wall. Lisa looked at me, curiously, her eyebrows stitching together. I beckoned her towards me with my finger.

She edged inside the cubicle, her back to the other wall. A tiny gap of air lived between our breasts. 'So we don't get interrupted again,' I whispered, and shut and locked the cubicle door.

The small lamp in the cubicle cast a shadow over Lisa, her eyes seeming more beautiful and pronounced than they had moments earlier. She lowered her head and looked at me through her long black hair.

I put my hand to her face, and with my index finger softly traced the line of her hair, from the top of her head, down the side of her face, over her shoulder and then inward towards the crease of her breasts. I opened out my palm, and took her whole breast in my hand, through her top, and gently squeezed it.

Lisa's lips parted and she let out a soft moan. I looked back to her face. Her eyes were now closed and her head was tilted back against the wall. I went up on tiptoes and kissed her open mouth, sticking my tongue deep inside and out again and then gently biting on her bottom lip.

I brought it towards me with my teeth, and then let it slide out again, the small natural cracks in her lip gliding over the edges of my teeth.

I moved to her neck, inhaled the sweet perfume that she wore, and began to kiss the skin between her shoulder and back. There was a nice taut firmness to the muscle above her shoulder, and I opened my mouth wide and tried to take the whole of it inside. Lisa gasped again and reached for my hands, which were now entwined in her hair, and then she brought them down to her breasts.

Our fingers were splayed across each other, and as I kissed her shoulder and held her breasts, she pulled down her top, letting them flow over the fabric in all their full-bodied glory. Instinctively, my mouth went towards her nipples, taking in their pert softness inside my lips, my tongue running over the small bumps that surrounded them.

Lisa put a hand through my hair and pulled it softly as her breathing became heavier. I began to squeeze her breasts harder and harder, enjoying the sensation of her flesh pouring out between my fingers.

I kissed and licked her nipple, then moved back to her mouth, taking her deep inside mine, then letting it go soft again, allowing her tongue to proceed into my mouth.

She pressed me back against the wall with both hands. She looked me deep in the eyes, as if to hold my attention there, as if she wanted me to stay focused on her eyes, so that I wouldn't see her hands as they travelled down my body.

She crouched slightly as her hand lifted up my dress. Her nail tickled my thigh as her fingers came back up, heading towards my pussy; my pussy, beating like a heart, desperate to be touched.

Her finger slipped inside the cotton of my panties, and tickled along the small line of hair. And then she teased past my clitoris, grazing it for a second, before going over to my other thigh. God, I thought, touch me, I want you to touch me there! Now!

And then she had lifted the dress up, and it was becoming bunched together, so I flicked off the straps and it fell gracefully to the floor. The motion must have inspired something in Lisa, because she put three fingers under the elastic of my panties, and pulled them down to the floor. On seeing my pussy, she let out a purr, like a satisfied cat, and began to nuzzle it with her face.

I felt my knees buckle slightly like a kind of spasm, and pressed my hand against the door to steady myself. Her tongue danced around my clitoris, pressing against it, then circling it, then pouncing on it, bringing the rest of her mouth with it, her lips pressed firmly against my pussy.

And then she shifted my legs apart, and seemed to go under me, and I shut my eyes and bit my lip, because there it was, her tongue, diving inside my vagina, inside me, its natural wetness mixing with the oily slickness that seemed to be dripping from me, as if I were melting, as if my very being were dissolving in some kind of ecstasy.

Lisa reached behind me and held my buttocks firmly in her hands, using her tongue inside and out. She began to lick in an upward motion, going from the very mouth of my pussy up to the clitoris and back down again. Each went slower than the last, so that the wait, the unbearable wait for her to reach my clitoris, became more painful . . .

Kiss it, I thought, suck it, my pussy screamed and, as though she had heard, she put her lips around my clitoris and sealed a hole with her lips. And then she sucked it into her mouth, pulled back on it, flicked her tongue over it, and I thought I might explode. I twisted my hands inside her hair and gritted my teeth, just as we heard the door to the ladies' open.

I froze. Someone had come in. I tried to exhale softly but my heart rate was far too fast, and I had to slow down my breathing.

I glanced down at Lisa. She remained crouched, her mouth still on my pussy, her eyes looking up at me mischievously. I put my hand over my mouth to stop myself from laughing, or breathing too loud, or making any kind of noise.

Whoever had come in was now at the sink. They turned on the tap, and we heard the sound of someone washing her hands. And as the noise was raised, Lisa moved her tongue over my pussy again, tracing the shape of my clitoris again. I nearly screamed. I looked down at her and put a finger to my lips.

Which, it turned out, was a bad idea, because she seemed to take it as a kind of challenge.

She moved her tongue again, this time in a figure of eight, treating my clit as the centre point of the shape, crisscrossing it. She began to build up a steady rhythm, and I couldn't help it, my eyes rolled back in my head, and I was gyrating towards her on the middle of the eight, making her press harder against me each time she got there.

And I was squeezing my mouth shut, trying not to let the sounds of ecstasy come bursting out, trying to regulate my breathing through my nostrils. The sound of the taps stopped, and the person outside shuffled her feet a little, then froze, as if she might be trying to listen.

At this point, Lisa thrust her tongue deep into my pussy, pointing the wet tip against my nub. My knees buckled and I slid down the wall, feeling my wetness come out over Lisa's mouth.

I wanted to come. I wanted to let it all out. I felt this great mountain of tension, deep in my muscles, and I wanted them all to burst. And I wanted it now.

The person outside knocked on the door and we froze.

'Is everything OK in there?' came an elderly voice.

Lisa snorted, her breath bumping against my clitoris.

'Fine,' I said, with the most authority I could muster, 'I just dropped my handbag.'

The woman outside paused. 'As long as you're sure . . .' she said.

'Absolutely,' I replied.

'Well, OK then,' she said, and after what seemed like a lifetime, finally made her way back outside. As soon as the door closed, Lisa rose up, her face slick with my juice, and kissed me thickly on the mouth. I smiled, my skin tingling all over and my leg muscles sore from standing.

I reached down between Lisa's legs to feel her pussy. It was completely shaved, and coated with a sticky warmth. I slipped a finger between her lips and let it feel around the opening to her inside. It was warm and bumpy and fresh and I wanted to go deeper, and from the sound of her moans, so did Lisa.

She pushed her hand against mine, making the palm of my hand press against her clitoris, and she rubbed it in a circular motion, biting into my neck as her breath became heavier.

And her pussy felt different from mine, it was thicker, it was juicier, it felt warmer than mine. I pressed harder against it and Lisa pushed her tongue into my mouth and moaned, and I began to change the rhythm, move it anticlockwise, then freeze, then go clockwise. And every time I changed directions, Lisa would groan and dig her teeth into my shoulder.

I knew it was making her crazy. I knew she wanted me to stick to the one rhythm. But I liked making her crazy . . .

I crouched a little, and brought my other hand down, put another finger inside her. Her pussy was moist and soft and I searched for a nub, but couldn't find one.

Instead, I circled my finger close to the opening, along the ridge where I made a beckoning motion, and she shook and rocked, and so I pressed harder and faster.

And then she shuddered. Her whole body rocked from top to toe, and I pulled my face back because I wanted to see this, I wanted to watch her face as she orgasmed, and it was so beautiful, so poetic; her eyes pressed tightly together, her mouth open just enough to see her teeth, so white against the red background of her salivating tongue, and I reached inside her again for the final moments, until she came to rest on my shoulder.

She smiled. She handed me my clothes and we giggled as I began to get dressed. I smoothed down my skirt, ignoring the dampness in my panties. We opened the door and snuck out. At the sight of our reflections, we both laughed. We looked like we had been dragged through haystacks, our cheeks flushed and our hair entangled in a complete mess.

Lisa smiled and said, 'Mission accomplished.' She kissed my shoulder and walked out the door.

I leaned against the sink, splashed water on my face and made myself presentable again. I stared into my eyes. There was something different about them. I felt . . . I don't know . . . I felt alive. All this had happened so fast and it was so liberating. I wanted to sustain this feeling of abandon. Why not, I thought. Why not?

I wanted to keep this feeling, this feeling of excitement, of life, of lust, of ever-increasing appetite.

There was so much to experience, I realized. My life had been so controlled up to this point, so scripted, and now, ahead of me was a whole road of unknown. And it was exciting.

I stepped out into the pub to find drunk people singing and lounging across each other. They didn't know what had happened to me, how could they know, and some of them smiled at me as I passed them by, and I thought, if only you knew . . .

Lisa was back behind the bar scrubbing a glass. She winked at me and I felt myself blush. A man's hand brushed past mine and I looked up to see the man from earlier, Lord Keatley. He leaned towards me and whispered in my ear, 'See you on Friday,' and then he walked away.

You don't know what you missed, I thought, and made my way outside to find Genevieve.

The air was now cold, and the fine hair on my arms stood up. I looked around, trying to find Genevieve, but I couldn't see her anywhere. The crowd had died down, and the bonfire was nothing but smouldering embers. I made my way over to the large swing in the hope of seeing her there, but it was occupied by someone else.

Samuel sat looking off into the distance. His head stayed forward, but his eyes swivelled towards me. My breath froze in midair and I was amazed that, even in the darkness, his eyes had a kind of penetrating depth to them, as if he could see right through me, as if, unlike everyone else, he could see exactly what I had just been doing.

I folded my arms, unconsciously protecting myself.

'Genevieve's gone home,' he said, bluntly.

'Oh,' I whispered, suddenly confused. Why would she leave me here?

'She had too much to drink. She told me to take you home.'

I stumbled a little and mumbled something like, 'Oh right, thank you.'

He stood up and surveyed the scene. Not looking at me, he said, 'Are you ready to go?' And I suppose I was but it all seemed so odd, like reality had punctured the perfect evening, but how could I refuse? I had no idea where I was, and here was this sullen, brutish man, clearly annoyed about having to drive me back.

'I can call a taxi,' I said, in an attempt at defiance.

'You won't get one,' he said. 'Come on.'

And then he did something I didn't expect. He held my arm. Well, he sort of grabbed it, just above the elbow, and led me out. As we passed through the pub, I looked for Lisa, but couldn't see her, and within seconds we were in the car park. He pressed the button for the alarm, and the lock of his Range Rover popped up.

I opened the passenger door and climbed inside. The car smelled of leather and wood and grass, and I pulled the seatbelt across my chest. I hoped he hadn't been drinking. He took his time getting around to his side of the car and I reflected on how long this journey would be.

We drove out of the car park in silence and then climbed on to the country lanes. The roads were pitch black, flanked by thick bushes and fields. The headlights painted the roads with about twenty metres of view. I looked out the window, and wondered if I should speak.

'Thank you for this,' I mumbled, and he smirked.

There was another minute of silence until he finally spoke.

'How are your feet?' he asked, not looking at me.

'Oh,' I smiled. 'They're fine, thank you. All better.'

'Good,' he said.

And then it was silent again, and I thought, I don't want this, I want to prove to him that I'm not some kind of idiot. Then I berated myself inside: why did I want him to like me?

'Genevieve tells me you still work with horses.'

'Yup,' he answered, blankly.

'Do you like it?'

'You should come and visit them,' he said, and I was so shocked by this moment, this small olive branch of an offer, that I looked across at him.

'I'd like that,' I said.

'Come tomorrow,' he said, pausing at a junction.

'I will,' I replied.

There was more silence to come, but this time it was a little more comfortable. I don't know if it was the drink, or my strange mood, or the darkness that enveloped us, but I felt like I could talk to him now.

'Genevieve told me about your wife. I'm so sorry.'

He stared ahead.

'Thank you.' He changed gears. 'It was a while ago now.'

He glanced at me.

'I heard you lost your boyfriend.'

'I didn't lose him,' I laughed. 'I had to get rid of him.'

'OK,' he smiled. 'How are you now?'

I looked across at him. I thought about it.

'Better,' I said, and I was.

We arrived at the gates to Genevieve's house.

I now wished the journey was longer.

Samuel came round and opened my door. He took my hand in his big rough hands and helped me down on to the gravel. I looked up at him. He stared back, but didn't flinch.

'Goodnight,' I said.

'Goodnight, naughty girl.'

Goose pimples rose again, so I turned and walked into the house as he drove away.

And when I got inside, Genevieve had left a note: 'I look forward to your report tomorrow . . .'

When I reached my room, my mobile phone vibrated under the bed. I had been without it since I had arrived here. I had made a conscious decision not to use it or check it or anything, and it actually surprised me to hear it buzzing. I picked it up.

It was a text message. From Henry. It read, 'I miss you.'

My heart plummeted. Damn you, Henry.

CHAPTER SIX

THURSDAY 11TH JUNE

Today was the strangest day I've had in the country yet . . .

The rain woke me up as it tapped against my window. I took a hot shower and got into some fresh clothes. I dried my hair and went down to the kitchen. Again, Genevieve was nowhere to be seen, so I helped myself to a croissant and had a large glass of fresh orange juice.

I sat leafing through a magazine for about an hour, then Genevieve popped her head around the door.

'Do you want to watch?'

I stood up on seeing her, and spluttered a good morning, but she ignored it and asked again.

'Do you want to watch?'

I asked her what she meant. She told me she had some clients in the office, a couple who were worried that they weren't satisfying each other. Both were tempted to stray, a lot, but neither wanted to break their 'special bond'. Genevieve had been working through these issues with them, and had come to a point where they had decided that they wanted to only make love to each other, but for there to be someone else in the room. A stranger. Watching them.

'They know me too well for this one. I was going to find someone for the next session, but . . . you're here.'

I blinked heavily a number of times. 'What?'

Genevieve smiled. 'You don't have to do anything. Just sit in the chair. And watch.'

Could this week get any crazier? I thought.

'I don't understand,' I said. 'They just want to have sex in your office?'

And then Genevieve smiled. 'It's not an office. It's an Exploration and Recreation Room.'

I murmured something about not feeling right and any other number of excuses, but my heart rate had already begun to increase and I knew that, no matter what I said, my interest had been piqued. If all I had to do was watch, how hard could it be?

'Will you be there with me?'

'No,' Genevieve answered. 'They want a stranger. Look, if you don't like it, you can stop at any time.'

And so I followed her into the corridor. I knew that if I didn't go right then, I would talk myself out of it, and given that I had come this far, I knew I wanted to keep going.

We arrived outside the office door and I could hear murmuring inside. I instinctively ran a hand through my hair, wanting to look as presentable as possible. Genevieve smiled at me. 'You'll be fine,' she whispered. 'But you have to be silent.'

'Why?' I whispered, and Genevieve winked.

And pushed the door open.

I don't know what I was expecting. I think I was expecting a middle-aged couple fully clothed, holding hands on a sofa. At most I expected to see that chaise longue I had glimpsed through the crack in the door.

What I found was so extraordinary that I think I actually said 'oh!' out loud. Genevieve wasn't lying. This was no office.

The room was much bigger than I expected. Like the Tardis. It was quite ornate, with big wooden carvings in the walls, showing scenes of ancient mythology, strange half-men half-bull creatures riding women and all sorts of weird imagery. At one end of the room were the chaise longue and two chairs that had clearly been moved aside.

In the middle of the room was a large, white, crisply made bed. It had four posts that came out of the corners about half a metre high. And tied to these posts was a woman, with a silk scarf fixed around her eyes. Her wrists were bound by purple silk ribbons that stretched around her forearms and pulled each arm to each post at the top of the bed.

She was naked except for a small pair of black panties. Her ankles were crossed over each other, and her head lay back against the pillows. Although the ribbons seemed very tight across her arms (she couldn't lay her wrists on the bed as they were suspended a little too high) her face remained still, staring up into the blindfold.

Standing by the bed was a tall man wearing a white shirt with no collar. The top few buttons were open, revealing a toned, tanned chest. His salt-and-peppery hair was thick and his stubbled face hid a warm and sensual mouth. On his legs he wore loose-fitting trousers.

I looked at him, my mind a complete vacuum of shock as he gazed back at me. He put a finger to his lips, and pointed towards the leather chair at the end of the room. I glanced back at Genevieve, who was watching through the door. She smiled again and closed it. Leaving me alone. With a blindfolded woman and a half-naked man.

I took a seat. The leather was soft and fresh-smelling. My jeans felt far too snug all of a sudden, and entirely inappropriate for this kind of atmosphere. I should have been wearing something softer. Something that could easily fall open.

The man smiled at me for a second, and I'm not sure if I smiled back. I think I tried to keep a blank face. After all, isn't that what a therapist would do? Try not to make any judgments. Let the client reveal themselves.

I folded my hands over my lap and tried not to think too hard. Tried to just let it happen. The bed was a good metre and a half in front of me so it felt strangely safe, almost like I was watching a play or something.

And so it began . . .

The man picked up a small, clear bottle. He popped open the top and climbed on to the bed. He kneeled over the woman and, from under his thighs, I could see her stomach muscles contract in anticipation. He raised the bottle up high and then tilted it forward.

Some drops of oil splashed against the pale skin of her arms. I could not see her face, but I heard her exhale quickly as if in surprise. The man moved the bottle across her chest, letting the oil splash against her round nipples. The oil spilled over on to her other arm and then the man stood up again and replaced the bottle on its stand.

With his back to me, he began to remove his shirt. As he pulled his arm out of the sleeve, the muscles in his back danced and bounced over each other and I felt my mouth go dry. I reached my tongue up against the roof of my mouth to try to lubricate it.

The man removed his trousers and dropped them to the floor, revealing firm, hairy, manly legs. He stood by the bed, only a pair of black cotton shorts hiding what appeared to be a growing cock.

He leaned over the bed and placed his palms on the woman's arms. He began to press the oil into her skin, sweeping his hands over her flesh, and pressing his thumbs deep into her muscles. His knee came on to the mattress and he raised himself up and over her again. This time his hands came down over her breasts, his fingertips circling her pink nipples that now stood erect, and then he squeezed them between his fingertips, before taking both mounds in his hands and pushing them together.

I watched as her ribcage began to rise and fall, deeper and more rhythmically than before. He put his hands together as if in prayer and then drew them down her stomach. He paused at her soft shell of a bellybutton and raised his little finger up, letting a drop of oil dangle off it, until it fell inside the smooth opening. He leaned down and kissed it with his lips, and I saw her whole body shiver.

As his face came up again from her stomach, he looked back at me. And I stared into his eyes and felt that tingle again, that tingle that had been present for most of this week, that tingle that now seemed so prevalent, so passionate, between my legs. He smiled at me and turned back to the woman. He moved up her body and kissed her on the mouth.

From my safe place in the chair, I could hear her soft, pleading moans, and I wanted to join her. Suddenly, it felt so frustrating to be sat here, to be wearing tight jeans, to not be naked and touching myself. From under my clasped hands, I let a finger touch the outside of my button fly and press against my clitoris. It felt good.

The man shimmied down the bed, until he was at its foot. He unclasped the girl's ankles and spread her legs, then reached up and delicately removed her panties. They dropped to the floor by the bed, and from where I was sitting I could see them glistening with her anticipation.

His hands pressed into the inside of her thighs, tracing the taut white muscle that peeked out. And then he put his face right down, right inside her, so that all I could see was the back of his head, and above it, those milk-white breasts as they rose and fell.

As his head began to move up and down, so too did the woman's breathing, now soft, now harder, now more lyrical and melodic, a tune of mmmmmm's being added to the release of air.

I noticed the flesh on her wrists as it pushed out from between the crossovers on the ribbon. She was straining at them, trying to break free, and I understood why. She wanted to grab on to something, anything, her breasts, his hair, anything, just to have the feeling of something in her hands, and I understood it completely, because I began to perspire, desperately wanting to delve inside my jeans and touch my pussy that was crying out for some attention. Stop this feeling, it cried, I need to be touched.

And then the man reared up. He removed his shorts, revealing a huge and powerfully erect penis. He kissed his way up her body, pausing to put her left breast into his mouth, and then he was kneeling over her chest, his cock firm over her blindfolded face. He angled himself, and then put it inside her mouth.

And I watched from behind as her pussy, peeking out at me, glistened and smiled and rubbed against the bed, as his buttocks clenched backward and forward as he gently pushed back and forth between her lips.

As he was completely turned away from me, I reached down and quietly popped the first few buttons of my jeans. I shifted in the chair a little, leaning myself back. Even just doing that, feeling my fingertips brush the top of my pussy was amazing.

The man removed his cock from her mouth, and then leaned over the bed to a table. He picked up a pair of scissors and with one solid slice, he cut the ribbons free. The woman brought her hands forward and put them behind the man's back.

He released himself from her and stood up again, then he put his hand on her side and helped her up on to her knees. She crawled gingerly down the bed.

Were it any different, she would have been staring right at me. Except that she was still blindfolded. I watched her face, her soft mouth open and wet. The man got on the bed behind her, his hard cock in his hand, and he looked at me looking at him. His lips parted in a half smile.

He glanced down at my hips. I had not noticed it. I was grinding softly against the chair. I don't know how long I had been doing it, but I had been instinctively moving my hips up and down against the leather, and when he noticed I was doing that, I thought maybe I should stop, but I couldn't help it. I was slightly overwhelmed, in lust, in need, and so I continued and the man nodded, and because he nodded, I reached down into my panties, placed my hand over my opening and slid a finger inside.

It slid in so perfectly, so warmly, like home, like right, like perfect, and I kept my eyes on the couple as he raised himself up, and entered her.

She put her face up, took a sharp intake of breath, and then he was penetrating her, slowly at first, and then faster, and harder, and I found my hand mimicking their movements, circling my clitoris and feeling for the nub faster and faster.

And he began to groan, but he wouldn't take his eyes off me, and I wouldn't let him, even though my eyeballs wanted to roll back, they wanted oblivion, but I held firm, watching him as he fucked her, harder and harder.

He lifted up her legs, and she came down on to her forearms, and he pulled her legs all the way behind him, and began to push deeper and deeper into her, and her face began to flush, and she moaned louder, and as the sound of their flesh slapping against each other grew, I wanted to join in their moans, but I had to be silent, I had to not be there, so I just kept touching and touching and trying to breathe softly while I watched.

Then he put her legs back down and pulled out of her, and, still staring at me, he let out a roar as his sperm flew from his cock and splashed on to her back in four thick streams. As each stream landed, she smiled and frowned and gasped, and then he was pressing against her, laying her down, his full weight on her back, kissing her neck and whispering, 'I love you.'

They lay there catching their breath and kissing, and now it seemed like I wasn't in the room any more, I wasn't part of it, but I wanted to finish, I needed more.

I buttoned myself up as quietly as I could and made my way to the door.

I had wanted to see her eyes.

I guess that wasn't allowed.

I quietly opened the door and made my way back to the kitchen. Genevieve smiled at me.

'You look like you've had fun.'

'I think they're finished,' I said, blushing, because I was still hot, I was still hungry, I still needed feeding.

Genevieve moved off down the corridor and I stood by the sink, pressing myself against the porcelain.

And, within moments it seemed, the man and woman appeared in the driveway at the window, fully dressed and looking refreshed, walking arm in arm to their car.

The woman glanced back and looked in the window at me. She smiled and turned away. She had beautiful sparkling green eyes. The couple kissed and climbed into the car.

I couldn't talk to Genevieve now, I needed to take care of myself. I couldn't concentrate on anything.

I raced up to the bathroom and lay on the soft floor. I plunged my hands between my legs, imagining the scene in the room, this time with both of them looking at me, their eyes sparkling as they fucked, and within seconds I had come.

CHAPTER SEVEN

In the afternoon I came downstairs, my head feeling strangely floaty. I wanted to take a walk. I didn't want to see Genevieve. And I wondered why that was. Was I embarrassed? Was I ashamed? Was I angry? I realized that it was none of those things.

The truth was that I was having too much fun. And I didn't want to analyze it. I knew that if I discussed things with Genevieve then I would lose something. Like when you blow a bubble with washing-up liquid and it looks so magical and it hangs in the air until you prod it softly with your finger and all you're left with is a soapy mess on the floor.

Fortunately Genevieve was in another session, and so the rest of the house was empty. I left her a note saying I'd be back later and stepped out of the patio door. The air was clear now and the sun had come out. The grass was damp but firm and I made my way down the field at the back.

I had no real plan – at least, I thought I didn't – I was just walking. It was only later that I realized the route I was taking was the same route we had walked as children. And that the destination of this route was Samuel's stables.

It was a lovely walk. The flat land stretched out miles into the distance, and each field was a different, more vibrant colour than the last. I walked through vast green-ness, and then crossed over into the startlingly yellow wheat, the notches of the flower scraping against my legs.

As I walked I tried not to think too hard, about Henry, about anything, about the fact that in a few days I would be returning to London and to work and to troubles. I wondered if I could stay here for ever and live a life of wild abandon like my friend Genevieve. It seemed such a pure life.

I wondered if I could mix the two. Take the lessons I was learning here and apply them in London. Not worry so much. Let things happen. Be open to life. To sex.

I took deep gulps of the scented air, took in the cut-grass smell of green and stretched my arms. Before I knew it I was by the fence that separated the field from the stables.

It was strange to stand here as I had over a decade ago. The fence was lower than I remembered but the stables themselves were still large and imposing. Some horses grazed out in a pen. I climbed between the two posts of the fence and stumbled awkwardly on the odd tufts of grass.

I could hear a horse whinnying from behind the big red doors. I was tempted to look for the old hole that we used to spy through. But I was a woman now. So I walked around to the large open doors.

Inside were two horses. One was stabled up and drinking water.

The other, a large black beauty of a horse was in the centre of the stables. Samuel was stood in front of it, gently tugging on its reins and making soothing sounds to it, trying to calm it. In his other hand he held some carrots, to which the horse eventually acquiesced and ate. Samuel, wearing black boots and dirty trousers, patted the horse, and said, 'There you go . . . there you go . . .'

I watched him for a moment. It was interesting to see him so gentle with the horse. He always came across as a brusque and rough man, but here he was treating the horse as if it were a child.

His strong forearms bulged out from the edges of his shirt as he tugged the reins a little harder and led the horse back into its stable. I now felt as if I had been watching for too long. And so I spoke.

'Is he misbehaving?'

Samuel didn't even flinch. Nor did he turn around to face me. Which made me wonder how long he had known I was standing there.

'*She*. She is fine. She had a fall in the winter. She's much better now.'

And once the horse was safely enclosed, he turned to me.

And didn't speak. Just stared at me with those rough, melancholy eyes. He looked rough and soft all at once. He dusted his hands together and the excess food and mud fell to the ground.

And then he asked me something that made me feel stupid for walking over there. I mean, hadn't he asked me to come last night?

'What do you want?' he said.

I blustered a little before responding, 'I don't know. I came to see the horses I guess.'

'Well, then,' he replied. 'You'd better take one for a ride.'

'Oh no,' I said, 'I haven't ridden in years. I don't know if I remember how.'

'But you have ridden before?' he asked, in a slightly mocking tone.

'Well, yes,' I replied, cockier than I had intended it to sound. 'Quite a lot actually. When I was younger.'

'Well then,' he nodded. 'You shouldn't have a problem.'

He disappeared for a moment and reappeared leading a horse by the reins. The horse was magnificent, a beautiful bay with a thick flowing mane. He turned away from me and secured the saddle. I stood back watching nervously. The truth was I hadn't ridden a horse since I was about twelve. I used to love them, but was thrown off one day and the experience had left me too rattled to want to try again. I began making excuses.

'I really should get back to Genevieve, she doesn't know where I am,' or something like that, but Samuel didn't seem to be listening. His eyes were scanning my lower body. I stared at him, wondering what he was doing. Then I realized. He was assessing my legs with his eyes. I felt very hot all of a sudden. He turned and adjusted the length of the stirrups.

And then he turned to me. 'Come here,' he said.

I stepped forward.

'Take the reins in your left hand.' I did. They were worn and leathery, like old furniture. 'Now with the same hand take hold of the saddle.' I stretched out for it. 'Now use your right hand to put your foot in the stirrup.' I felt awkward, not wanting to stumble or make myself look stupid. 'Now reach up with your right hand to the back of the saddle and flex your knees. On three. One.' I tensed my legs. 'Two.' I took in a breath. 'Three!'

Out of nowhere I felt his hands on my hips. They gripped me firmly, like foundations holding up a bridge. And then, with surprising ease, he lifted me up and on to the horse. In his hands I felt weightless.

'This is Chocolate Davison,' said Samuel and patted his mane. The horse felt heavy beneath me . . . solid. I felt nerves trickle over me. It felt normal, familiar to be on top of a horse. My young body had been used to the sensation. But it also remembered that fall. I held tightly to the front of the saddle and smiled nervously down at Samuel. He walked over to the wilder of the two horses, brought her out and mounted her.

'Relax,' he said. 'They can feel it if you're anxious and then they take advantage.'

That made me feel no better.

He looked at me again. 'You look fine up there. You've got a good seat and your heels are well down.' I shook my head a little and exhaled. 'Just remember to press yourself down into the saddle and squeeze with your thighs.' He paused before moving off. 'But you know all this anyway…'

I berated myself as I felt my cheeks redden again.

I pressed my calves gently into Chocolate's hide, and we moved out into the field at a small trot. The horse rose and fell beneath me, its back and sides pulsating beneath my legs. 'Easy,' called out Samuel as he came after us.

He pulled up alongside us on his mighty beast. We hacked out for five minutes or so and I wondered why I had been so nervous . . . this was lovely. The air seemed fresher at this height; it filled my lungs with deep bracing waves. And to feel the horse beneath me, carrying me, holding me, as we rode across the earth, was something I realized I had missed.

I was aware that Samuel was watching me the whole time, assessing me, measuring me, working me out.

Suddenly he called out. 'Follow me,' he shouted and shot off into the distance at a canter. Chocolate reared a little, and I panicked for a moment, pulling back on the reins.

I looked across the vista at Samuel way ahead. *Dammit*, I said to myself, muttered a little prayer, then shortened the reins. Chocolate bolted forwards and I squeezed my thighs against the saddle.

My hair swished and blurred my vision as the wind whipped through it. The sound of the hooves belting along the ground rose up into the whistling air. We came up close to Samuel as he slowed his horse down. He pulled back arriving next to us at a small clop.

'How was that?'

'Amazing,' I breathed, secretly thinking, *terrifying . . .*

'Try not to be so stiff,' he said. 'Try to move with the rhythm of the horse. It will be more comfortable. Remember to sit deep in the saddle and let your hips move with the horse.' He moved ahead again, and this time I focused on his body as it rode up and down on the horse. As I watched he stood up in the saddle like a jockey so that I could see his buttocks rise then clench, balancing on his strong thighs, his arms pulsing through his shirt. I pressed down harder in the stirrups and, without loosening the grip of my thighs, relaxed from the waist down to move with the horse. I was beginning to feel more in control.

And as I matched Chocolate's rhythm, it all clicked into place, suddenly it was thrilling and we overtook Samuel and raced ahead.

The Fens out here are so flat, so marvellous that you can see far, far into the horizon and I set my sights on that horizon and off we went, whizzing through the air, as it zipped past us, leaning forward now so that my hair flapped over the horse's, and I felt wild at last, untethered, unabashed, strong and free.

I heard the thunder of Samuel's horse's hooves as he raced behind us, and within a moment, I felt the wind change next to us, and he was in front again. I leaned back into the saddle and became aware of the sensation of it as it pressed against me. It felt good. I pressed down on the horse, and as the saddle rose and fell, it rubbed against my clitoris, stimulating my whole body.

As the air stung my skin, the warmth between my legs spread and I looked ahead, watching the taut muscles on Samuel's back as they held back the beast with amazing control.

We rode like this for what seemed like an hour, but really couldn't have been more than a few minutes, when Samuel called out and we calmed our pace until we found ourselves back at the stables.

Samuel reached for my hand, but I slid off all by myself and stood in front of him, our cheeks flushed. 'Thank you,' I said. 'I needed that.'

He looked back at me and smiled, really, I think, for the first time. 'I could tell.'

I walked back towards the door. 'How long are you staying for?' he asked.

'End of the week,' I said.

He turned back to the horses and started to lead them away.

'I'll see you again,' he said, and off I went.

Genevieve and I ate together tonight and drank wine and laughed and talked about nothing sexual or prescient, but we talked about movies and music and stories from our schooldays, and it was all quite relaxing.

I took a hot bath to soothe my muscles, which ached from the horses.

And now I'm going to sleep. Very well, I think . . .

Tomorrow night we have a party to go to. Genevieve says it is my final mission. Which I find odd, because I think I'm already cured. I've done everything she asked. I feel . . . changed. I feel restored. Alive. Ready for the world. What will this party hold that I have not yet experienced?

This is what I've learned. There is nothing I can do, as tomorrow is all unknown. So I'll have to wait and see what all the fuss is about . . .

CHAPTER EIGHT

FRIDAY 12TH JUNE

Tonight was, without doubt, the most thrilling, most strange, most confusing, most amazing night yet.

Genevieve took me to a spa today, and we had a massage and a manicure and a pedicure and generally spoiled ourselves. We had a nap after lunch and then I spent the afternoon in the bath. I honestly can't think of a more decadent day than that.

About six o'clock, she called me into her bedroom and we decided what to wear that evening for the party. I showed her another floral-print dress I had brought and she shook her head.

'Tonight is special,' she said.

'What exactly is it?' I asked.

'Well . . .' she smiled.

She explained that it was a private party. That there was a secret collection of people in the locality who once every couple of months indulged in what they described as 'an evening to blow out the cobwebs'. What this apparently meant was that the select few, many of them former clients of Genevieve, would get together for a night of sexual frolics.

'Is it an orgy?' I asked.

And Genevieve answered as only a therapist would – with a question: 'Would you like it to be?'

I felt butterflies in my stomach as I imagined horrible hordes of hairy men rutting and sweating. I think Genevieve noticed the change in me and she said softly, 'You don't have to do anything you don't want to.'

She picked out a tight black basque, with stockings and handed them to me. 'Wear this underneath,' she said. 'You'll look gorgeous.' And then she passed me a tight-fitting black ball gown with a white rim that emphasized the cleavage. 'I'll help you get into it.'

I let my dressing gown fall to the floor, and stood in front of the mirror. How far had I already come, to be able to stand naked in front of another human being, albeit someone I cared deeply about. The full-length mirror stared back at me, and behind me I could see Genevieve's eyes glance over my body.

'Here,' she said, and handed me the basque. Genevieve reached forward and fixed the clips together on my back. The fit was snug, forcing my breasts to spill over the top a little. Clips hung down from my waist. I went over to the bed and rolled on the silk stockings.

'You look amazing . . .' said Genevieve.

'Should I wear a thong with this?' I asked.

'No,' she said. 'Don't wear anything.'

I stepped into the ball gown. The bodice was fitted and then the dress flowed out towards the legs, elegant, classy and extremely Audrey Hepburn-esque. Genevieve gave me some long black opera gloves to finish it off – the look was complete. I had to admit, I felt gorgeous.

Genevieve put on her outfit, a slinky red silk number, complete with stockings and heels, then she straightened my hair.

Finally we stood before the mirror, our arms round each other's waists. Quite a pair, I thought. For the first time in my life, I felt like Genevieve's equal. It was a good feeling.

The taxi wound through the country lanes. The driver couldn't take his eyes off the two of us as we giggled in his rear-view mirror.

Lord Keatley's house was magnificent. A long lane curled down a gravel path to arrive at a huge ornamental palace, lit up at the front by large white lights; a succession of people, all dressed up to the nines, were making their way inside to escape the moonlight.

We stepped on to the drive and the gravel crunched beneath our heels. As we began to ascend the large marble steps to the entrance, Genevieve grabbed my arm and stopped me.

'Do you want to know what your final mission is?'

I stared into her beautifully made-up face.

'What is it?'

'You've come a long way this week . . . you've done things you didn't know you wanted to do. And now, your final mission . . . is to do whatever you want to do. Tonight, like the rest of your life, is yours.'

She kissed me on the cheek and I grinned at her.

'Come on,' I said, and we walked to the big door.

A butler was there to greet us. On his arm he carried a basket. Inside the basket were a series of masks. He reached in and handed us two, one white and one black. 'Ladies, these are for you. Enjoy the summer ball,' he said.

I held the mask in my hand. It was delicate porcelain with a ribbon around the back to tie round your head. I placed its cool surface on my skin. It covered my eyes and the tip of my nose. Interesting, I thought, and, once Genevieve had secured hers, in we went.

The hallway was draped in black curtains, each studded with small star lights. At the end of the hallway were a number of staircases leading in different directions. Above the staircases was a sign. It read,

WELCOME TO THE MIDSUMMER MASKED BALL. THERE ARE MANY PLACES TO EXPLORE. PLEASE ENJOY YOURSELF. AND IF YOU DON'T FIND WHAT YOU ARE LOOKING FOR, THEN YOU ARE IN THE WRONG PLACE . . .

Genevieve chuckled. She reached over to a silver platter and picked up two champagne glasses. 'Here,' she said, 'You'll need this.' We clinked the two flutes together and drank back the cool, pink champagne.

'Where shall we go?' I asked.

'Pick a staircase,' she replied.

I chose the right-hand one, and we walked up it. As we approached the top, we could hear the sound of muffled music coming from behind a door. The door, which was slightly open, revealing some flashing lights, beckoned us forward. 'Are you ready?' whispered Genevieve. 'Ready as I'll ever be,' I said, and pushed open the door.

No one turned to look our way. And I don't blame them. Everyone's attention was fixed on the centre of the room. People sat on ornate chairs in neat rows around the middle as if they were watching a classical performance or something. They sipped their champagne and smiled.

The music that blared out of the speakers was a kind of track I can only describe as classical techno. A sort of recognizable piece of music (maybe I knew it from an advert?) remixed and played out to a thumping beat.

Genevieve squeezed my hand, and we took a seat near the back.

I already felt my heart rate increasing as we took in the scene.

A woman, fit, toned and sensual, danced in the centre. She threw long ribbons in the air and caught them, and span and leaped and fell and twisted and turned. It was almost like a ballet, the grace of her body reflecting the melody of the music. But there was a difference.

She was completely naked. And while she danced and leaped and fell, a man with leather belts strapped around his muscles cracked a whip on the floor. If the woman ever dropped one of the ribbons, the man would crack his whip and she would crawl towards him along the floor, pouting. When she reached the man, he would slap her bottom with an open palm and then kiss her full on the mouth.

She would then get up and begin to dance again. Again she would drop the ribbon and again the whip would crack.

The lights were out, except for a red and a blue spotlight that swirled sensuously around the room. I glanced around me, trying to make out the other guests.

Everyone was in dinner suits, black tie, or dresses, and the way they watched the show was with deadpan, slightly sleepy faces. I frowned at Genevieve and whispered, 'What the hell is this?' She laughed and answered, 'This is nothing . . .'

The lights went out and the music seemed to get louder. Suddenly a flame filled the air, and as the lights came back on, I could see the man was blowing a flame on to two *poi* that hung from long lines. He handed them to the woman who began to twirl and spin the flaming *poi* around her body. The flames skimmed her breasts and some of the people in the audience took in an audible breath.

'This really doesn't do it for me,' whispered Genevieve, and I couldn't help but agree. We stood up quietly and left, shutting the door behind us.

The hallway was echoey quiet and a butler arrived at the top of the stairs. He handed us two more flutes of champagne and we giggled and wandered along the hallway, then down a smaller set of stairs.

As we approached a door, a man came out. It was Lord Keatley. He nodded when he saw us. 'Good evening, ladies,' he said. We said hello and he kissed Genevieve on the lips. She pulled away and he came towards me, trying to kiss me too. I moved my face so that his lips landed on my cheek, and he added, 'Hope you enjoy yourselves.'

We thanked him and, as he walked away, rolled our eyes at each other. We went into the room, and what was inside was even more extreme.

The whole room was painted black. There were iron bars made up into the shape of a cube, resembling a kind of cage. Inside the cage were a man and a woman. The man had a rubber mask over his head, with a zip where his mouth should have been. The woman wore a latex red dress with holes cut into it, where her breasts poked out.

They were both strapped to the bars by chains that cut across their arms and legs. They were literally hanging by their wrists. A small group of people stood around them as one man and one woman systematically whipped them. They both let out groans. Another man sat in a darkened corner, his trousers gone, his hand frantically pulling on his penis.

I stepped straight out of the room with Genevieve. 'Oh my God,' I said, and laughed, because there didn't seem anything else to do.

Then Genevieve spoke. 'Let's split up.'

I didn't want to at all. I was beginning to think that this really wasn't the kind of party I wanted to be at, and the thought of not having Genevieve next to me made it even less appealing.

'I think you need to explore this place without me. That way you can find something you like all by yourself.'

'But what if I don't like any of it?'

'Then you don't have to like any of it. And we can go home. Honestly, sweetheart, it's up to you.'

I said OK, and we agreed to meet up in a couple of hours if we didn't bump into each other.

I made my way back towards the ground floor and followed the sound of music coming from the back of the house. Out through a large kitchen were big glass doors that opened on to the garden. In the garden was a large marquee, and Rat Pack music was playing inside.

I walked towards it, trying to imagine what horrors I would find within. But when I stepped inside I saw much more of what I had originally expected. Here was a group of people, dancing on a makeshift dance floor, fully dressed, smiling, enjoying themselves as they glided around the floor.

I breathed a sigh of relief. There were chairs along the edges and I took one and sipped my champagne. I watched the couples dance and thought for a moment. A middle-aged couple, exquisitely dressed, spun round and held each other and smiled, and I marvelled at the genuine warmth they seemed to have for each other.

I began to think again about couples. About the concept of couples. About Henry. I wondered how long these two had been married, and if they were always this happy.

A man in his forties sat down next to me. He wore a tuxedo, which already seemed ruffled. He was slightly out of breath.

'Oh my goodness, do you mind if I sit?' he said.

'Not at all . . .'

He asked who I had come with and I told him, my friend, and he said he had come with his wife. 'Where is she?' I asked.

'Upstairs somewhere,' he said. 'She'll be back in a minute.'

We chatted for a while. I couldn't help feeling uncomfortable. The fact that here was this perfectly pleasant, perfectly normal man, being quite jovial, and yet his wife, who he said he had been married to for seventeen years, was 'upstairs'. I knew what was upstairs. I had seen it. Didn't he mind?

He paused and leaned forward on his chair. 'Would you like to go upstairs with me?'

I looked at the dance floor. 'No, thank you,' I answered, as politely as I could.

'You'd enjoy it,' he said.

'So everyone keeps telling me.'

'Well . . . never mind. I hope you enjoy the dancing, very nice to meet you,' he concluded, and he was gone.

How fucking weird was this evening?

I resisted the urge to bolt and tried to concentrate on the couples dancing again. It was real to some extent and for that I was grateful.

After a while I stood up and was about to make my way out when a man, his black tie loose and his top button undone, came towards me. And I felt the hair at the back of my neck stand on end. Because it felt like salvation.

It was Samuel.

He walked brusquely up to me, took my wrist in his big hand, spun me around and led me to the dance floor. Before I knew what was happening, I was twirling and pirouetting to the sound of Frank Sinatra. I smiled, because this was nice, if odd, and I was glad to see a familiar face. The music slowed and Samuel pulled me in close to him. My face turned sideways and pressed against his shoulder.

I could smell his skin. It gave an aroma of spice and wood and man. He rocked me gently from side to side, his other hand pressed into the small of my back.

'Are you having fun?'

'I am now,' I said.

'I know what you mean. It's nice to see a real person here.'

And then we danced in silence until the end of the song. When it finished, I curtsied, and he smiled and then led me off the dance floor. 'I'm going to go back to the house,' he said. 'I need to use the bathroom.' And before I could protest or say that I would come to the house with him, he was gone.

Hmm, I thought, and stepped outside the marquee. The air was fresh, and filled with voices and music and drums. I stepped along the path and back towards the kitchen. Inside, waiters were preparing lavish silver dishes of caviar and oysters and crabs.

I grabbed a mini-bite, ate it, then dabbed at my lips with a napkin. The dancing and the air had sobered me up, so I took another glass of champagne, and followed a group of elegantly dressed women up the right-hand staircase. The lighting in this hallway was dim but warm. The women went ahead towards another room, but I could see steam coming from another door and found myself too curious not to look.

I stepped inside. The room was lit by what seemed a hundred little candles. In the centre was a large hot tub. It bubbled and steamed. There were three people in it, two men and a woman, but they didn't notice me come in.

They were too engrossed in each other. And I could understand why.

There was a bench in the corner of the room, which I sat on and let the steam hide me from their eyes. I rested my glass down and settled back. This was nice.

The two men were fairly well built, with short blond hair. The woman was older, but still well toned, her breasts bobbing above the water, her tight nipples peeking through the bubbles. One of the men was leaning down and sucking her breasts. The other man was behind her, kissing her neck and reaching down in front of her between her legs. She was moaning and trying to turn round to kiss the man behind her. The bubbles squeaked and popped over the moans, and then the man in front lifted up her body and turned her over.

Now the man who had been kissing her neck was facing her. She straddled him, and he put his arms around her back and pulled her in close. She put her tongue into his mouth, and their faces swayed over each other. The man behind her leaned in and ran his fingers through her hair, pulling it and kissing her neck.

For the first time that evening, I felt excited. And I wasn't quite sure why. But now that I think about it, I realize that the fantasy that had first made me come, the image I had replayed in my mind, was of a woman, me, surrounded by flesh, enveloped by skin, and here I was witnessing it first-hand.

I pressed further into the bench to feel some contact between the surface and my pussy.

The man behind now lifted the woman up at her waist, and positioned her hips downward. A deep groan followed, as her pussy must have slid on to the cock of the man in front of her. She twisted her head round and kissed the man behind, while the other started to move her up and down on him.

The water began to splash around the edges of the tub and the faster their motion became the more it splashed. The man behind stood tall for a moment, and I could see his cock poking out of the surface of the water. He reached over to the side and ripped open a condom. The woman purred as he slid it over the shaft.

He put his hands under the water. I watched as the woman squirmed and jiggled and gasped. And then he must have entered her because they all moved as one, all connected in that moment, in one three-sided shape. Their lips, hands, faces, chests, pussy and cocks all inter-mingling under the water, like something primordial, their bodies pulsating and writhing in tune with one another, their moans rising in chorus with each other.

The man on the bottom seemed to yelp and he gripped on to the woman's back, before slowing down, then the man behind stopped moving, clenched his face together and then rocked forward. The woman exhaled dramatically and, within moments, they had fallen out of each other and sat sweaty, exhausted and hot, their backs to the wall of the Jacuzzi, their heads leaned against the sides.

And they laughed and giggled and stared off into space, the two men slapping used condoms back on to the sides of the tub.

I knew it was time to move on, so I kept my head down, hoping the steam would cover my exit, and made for the door.

When I arrived in the hallway, I heard a bell and the sound of people moving towards one location. It was a kind of gong being sounded, over and over. Curious, I followed the sound until it brought me towards a set of double doors. Outside the doors were a whole row of dressing gowns, maybe forty of them. There was a sign in gold lettering that said, 'Help yourself'.

I put my hand on the door handle and entered.

Inside were maybe sixty people. And forty of them were having sex. Just all over the floor. Men and women and women and men, fucking each other. It was the most extraordinary sight I had ever seen.

There were mattresses and beanbags and sofas and chairs and nearly all of them were made up with naked and half-naked couples some oiled, some wet, all fucking. I literally didn't know what to do with myself and so I went and sat on one of the few empty chairs I could find.

I tried to survey the scene, to force it to make some sort of sense in my mind, but it was all too much. Mouths open and screaming, twisted, lips kissing, breasts in hands, cocks in pussies, skin against skin, twisting shapes around other skin, hair flapping up and down, and sweat pouring from every face.

I blinked heavily. Tried to focus on one thing. A woman straddling a man, her eyes closed as she ground herself down on to his hips, each thrust deeper than the last. She tilted her head back and splayed her hand over his chest. And as she came, her stomach flinched as if all the muscles inside had suddenly been electrocuted, and she must have made some kind of noise but it was lost in the meld of everything else.

I became aware of how ridiculous I must have looked, in this ball gown and these gloves, totally cloaked up in a sea of nakedness. And then I saw Lord Keatley across the room. He too was still fully dressed, leaning against the wall, his eyes brimming with the sex in front of him, and I wondered if he had noticed me there, this black silk ship in a sea of naked flesh.

Of course he hadn't. He was as lost as everyone else.

My eye was caught by a flash of red, as two women placed a long scarlet dildo between themselves, then held each other's shoulders as they bounced closer and closer to one another.

A man came up from between a woman's legs, his beard glistening with her wetness, his eyes sparkling with lust.

An oiled woman lay flat against an oiled man and slid up and down his chest, his cock lodged firmly inside her.

A woman and two men sat cross-legged, all three leaning forward, their tongues pointed out as they kissed each other in the centre of the circle. Their hands remained tight behind their own backs and it became clear that the only way to play that game was to use your tongue.

A woman held herself above a man, as she lowered her asshole onto his cock. He winced as she brought herself down on him and she smiled as he came.

Condoms littered the floor in silver buckets, and tubes of lubrication lay all about the place. It was like something out of Ancient Rome. I had no idea this sort of thing existed and I couldn't believe I was actually here to witness it.

It was intoxicating watching all this sex. I felt like my brain had kind of exploded because I couldn't make any sense of it, I couldn't make any judgment. There was just too much. On the one hand I found it amazing, even beautiful, that all these people could find this, to find a way to be so open and comfortable to behave like this, and on the other hand I found it totally bewildering. How does something like this even start, I wondered.

And yet I couldn't stop watching.

Then I caught a glimpse of Lisa, the barmaid. I spotted her lips first. They were curved into a solid O shape. She was on her hands and knees, while another girl, wearing a strap-on dildo, clutched her hips and thrust into her.

I looked at her face, and felt faintly wistful about the crazy encounter we had had together. It can't compete with this, I thought. As the girl pushed faster and faster into Lisa, I felt the need to leave, as if, perhaps, I shouldn't be watching this one.

Perhaps that's what Genevieve meant when she wanted us to separate. This kind of thing probably only works with strangers. With people you know there seems to be some kind of boundary. I don't know why.

I tried to pick my way across the room, without treading on anything or anyone! But as I got to the door, a gnarled hand reached out for my forearm. It was Lord Keatley.

'I'm so glad you came,' he said. 'Would you like to join me on the bed?'

'No, thank you,' I blurted, suddenly very, very keen to leave.

'I wish you would. I am the host, after all . . .'

'No, thank you,' I repeated, as firmly as I could, then wrenched my arm free and headed straight out the door.

I closed it behind me and breathed a sigh of relief. Lord Keatley had shaken me a little. Well, perhaps that whole surreal scene had shaken me. I was aroused, and confused, and tired, and now alone.

I wandered back down another corridor. And then another. And then another.

I seemed to have got myself lost. My heels echoed along the marble floors. Every time I found a staircase it only seemed to lead to another one.

At last there was a corridor that led to a window. There was someone leaning against the window, his figure in silhouette. It was Samuel. He stood with his hands in his pockets, his shirt now open by three buttons. He leaned back and smiled when he saw me.

'I lost you,' I said. I expected him to respond, but he didn't. He just stared at me, the moonlight illuminating his thick hair.

I walked close to him. I could make out his face more clearly now. His lips. Fixed. Still. Not giving anything away.

I stepped closer.

Still he stared at me. Then his gaze traced my body from toe to head. He narrowed his eyes a little. I felt naked.

He leaned forward and kissed me on the lips. And as those big rough lips pressed against mine, I felt a powerful jolt of electricity pass between us. He pulled back and I saw his eyes look down at my chest.

Suddenly his hands were on my hips, just like they had been at the stables. He roughly spun me around. I gasped a little in shock, and he steadied me. He ran his finger along my neck and again I felt goose bumps. He traced the curve of my shoulder to the top of my dress. And with one quick move he had unclipped it.

He turned me back round and the dress came away in his hands.

Placing the dress on one side, he looked at me in my basque. I stared back at him, nervous and excited. I looked him straight in the eye, like I had when I was a child. I wasn't going to let him see my nerves.

He lunged forward, scooped me into his arms and kissed me full on the mouth. His tongue prised apart my lips and was inside, diving and exploring and teasing, and his stubble scraped against my lips and chin and it was so wonderful because it was so manly. He lifted me up like a rag doll and placed me on a dresser by the wall.

He pressed his face into my chest, kissing and licking and grabbing my breasts, reaching behind me to unclip the top of the corset, until my breasts spilled over the top, into his waiting mouth. He grasped them and held them and touched them, and ran his tongue in circles over my nipples.

I felt my head get lighter and my pussy begin to moan again. This, it seemed to be saying, this is what you've wanted . . .

And then I remembered. I wasn't wearing any panties. His hand moved down my body, past the corset and he pushed it forward, groping for my opening. His finger slid down the groove, parting the lips and circling the entrance. And before I could gasp or exclaim or anything, his head was between my legs, sucking and pulling and probing at me, and I grabbed on to his hair, scared that I might explode off this dresser and go into orbit.

His fingers and tongue and teeth circled my clitoris and he pushed inside me with his fingers, instinctively feeling for the nub, and I shuddered as he tickled it, and now I was tearing at his shirt, wanting it off, wanting to see him before me in all his glory.

He stood up and ripped the shirt from his shoulders, revealing his taut muscular frame, and he picked me up again, and put me on my feet, my heels long gone, only my stockings and gloves remaining.

I kept the gloves on as I unzipped his trousers, letting them drop to his ankles. He kicked the trousers away and grabbed my breasts with both hands, pushing them together. I reached inside his shorts, stroking down the length of his long hard penis. It was large and firm and seemed to be straining against the shorts, and so I freed it.

The cock stood tall at a high angle, daring me to touch it, daring me to deal with it, and so I took it in both my hands. I slid the gloves up and down the shaft, and then just as I was about to kneel down, a voice interrupted us.

'Oh, *there* you are . . .'

I looked over and there was Genevieve. Standing in the corridor. She was leaning against a pillar, her arms folded delicately. The moonlight through the window gave her a slightly ethereal glow.

Samuel and I stared back at her, both frozen to the spot with surprise. My hands remained fixed around his cock. Genevieve walked slowly towards us, reaching behind herself to unzip her dress. As she continued to walk, the dress fell away from her, revealing her wonderful slim body underneath.

She arrived in front of Samuel and put her hand behind his head. His face remained passive, staring back at her. She kissed him, and he responded. And then she turned to me. She looked at me curiously, the light gleaming off her eyes.

'I didn't want to be left out,' she whispered.

And with that she kissed me. It was the kind of kiss I hadn't experienced since Henry, a kiss full of passion and care and love. Her lips melded with mine, slipped over and under them, taking my bottom lip between her teeth and gently tugging it towards her.

I opened my eyes and looked to Genevieve and Samuel. His cock remained thick and angled upward. Genevieve looked me in the eye as she reached down and took his cock in her hand. Samuel reached in front of Genevieve and grabbed my wrists. He slowly peeled off my gloves, bringing my hands to his face and kissing my palms.

Then he grabbed my hair and pulled me in close to kiss him. Genevieve ducked down between us and began to lick my nipples with soft circles of her tongue. Samuel's mouth seemed to envelop mine, I felt swallowed whole, disappearing into a cave of lust, of release.

Genevieve stood up again and put her hands on my waist. Samuel stepped back for a moment and watched us. I could see him out of the corner of my eye as Genevieve devoured my neck with her wet mouth. I began to moan quite heavily, and as I write this now I realize this was the only opportunity I had had all week to really let go, to not be afraid or embarrassed.

And so as I pushed Genevieve against the window, enjoying the feel of her buttocks splayed against the glass, I let out more groans. It was thrilling to be so vocal, to let out the need, to expel it, to sing . . .

And then Samuel's hands were on my bare shoulders, his fingers skimming my neck and then following my spine down to the top of my bottom, to the part where it swelled, and he was down again, biting roughly into my flesh, and I yelped for a moment, until he spun me over again. Now Genevieve was holding me from behind and he was tearing into me with his tongue, pushing aside the wet folds and staking a claim to the nub, digging in as far as he could and then running a lap of honour around the crease.

And I may have screamed with pleasure and delight, but then Genevieve had her fingers in my mouth, and I sucked them, then twisted towards her to kiss her mouth. It was becoming claustrophobic in this corner, squeezed between these two beautiful people, one big and strong, the other lithe and supple.

But the image from my mind began to meld with this, and here I was, where I wanted to be, surrounded by flesh, submerged in flesh, drowned in flesh. Here I was . . . at the centre of the pleasure.

Samuel slid a condom on to his cock, slid it down like a slick skin, which only served to make it more impressive, more top heavy, more ready to explode from its bulging head.

He lifted my legs up and apart. I automatically swung my ankles around the back of his waist, crossing them together. Genevieve's arms slipped under my armpits to caress and hold my breasts, sneaking an extra kiss from Samuel as he guided himself inside me.

His cock pushed through in one slow gorgeous movement, as if my insides were expanding just for him, accommodating him, welcoming him in with a champagne reception, embracing him, begging him to stay and to explore and to fill the place.

He began to rock back and forth, his right hand holding my bum as he pushed inside me. I began to mumble and speak, and God knows what I said, but I know if I could have articulated it, it would have been something like, 'thank you . . . and please don't ever stop'.

Genevieve began to moan with me, and brought one hand round my waist to my clitoris, which she rubbed in a circle, her nail tickling the hooded part and teasing it from the outside. Samuel closed his eyes momentarily and grabbed each of my buttocks, while I held steadfastly to his shoulders, and then he was moving faster and faster, the head of his cock opening and brushing the nub, scraping it and worshipping it, and I yelped and yelped like an overexcited animal.

And we were like animals. This great beast of a man, holding me off the ground while he ploughed into me, this smaller animal behind, scrabbling for some of the affection. I opened my eyes, wanting to stop myself from coming too soon, wanting to savour every second, to remember each minutiae.

I looked through my half-opened eyes at Samuel and he stared back at me, his mouth pulled tight as he groaned and huffed and puffed.

He put me down on to my feet and pulled back a little, letting his raging cock slip out of me with a small pop. He rounded on Genevieve who reached round and down, grabbing his wet shaft in her hand. She slipped it between her fingers, then licked her hand.

He turned her around and pressed her hands against the wall, in a crucifixion pose. She groaned as he pushed his cock inside her from behind, pressed his whole weight into her as he lay his body on to hers. Her face was turned towards the window and, as he pumped into her, she moaned on each thrust.

I leaned against the cabinet, my fingers inside my pussy – there was no patience here – and I watched them and wanted more and held my other hand on

Samuel's chest, feeling the muscles tilt and rise through his skin.

Genevieve reached for my hand and pulled it down between her legs. She pressed my fingers over her clitoris and showed me how she liked it, how she wanted it, circular and firm but never actually pressing the button, just skimming the edges. I followed her hand with my own, until she took it away, leaving me to it, and I watched her gorgeous face as she bit her lower lip, her face against the wall, while Samuel ground away behind her. I rocked back, touching myself with my other hand and trying to synchronize our rhythms.

Samuel bent over and stuck his tongue into my mouth and as he did, I increased the speed of my hands until Genevieve let out an almighty scream, and Samuel held her against the wall, pressing her bum down, making the clitoris touch the wall, and she struggled and smiled and exhaled and caught her breath . . . and blushed.

Samuel stepped down from her, sliding out one final time. Genevieve turned to face him, and dropped to a crouching position. She reached for his cock and put it into her mouth, sucking off her own taste, savouring the flavour of all this excitement, of all this adrenaline.

Then Samuel grabbed my wrists and pulled me down to the floor. I went on to my hands and knees, the cold marble surprising against my burning skin. And as he held me in both hands by the small of my back, I felt his cock, definitely on its final journey, push down and down, deep into my cunt, searching for one last taste of the nub.

I lowered my head to give him more of an angle, and he pushed and pushed, deeper and deeper, and my eyes rolled into my head, and I was lost, gone, amazed, exhilarated, and I felt him pull me towards him, and hold me tight, all arms and hands, and then his body convulsed in five clean jolts and on each jolt he dug his fingers into my flesh, and it felt good to feel this, to feel taken, to feel devoured.

He held me on the floor, his cock still firm inside me, and I rocked on it, pushed my full weight into it and ground down, until my insides shook and jumped and my whole body blushed a crimson red. I must have screamed louder than ever because even Genevieve let out a giggled, 'shhhh!'

We all sat for a moment, out of breath, confused, exhausted, our limbs entangled, our hair dishevelled to the point of disastrous. Genevieve leaned forward and pulled the condom off Samuel's cock. She grabbed my hand and pulled me closer to it, then the two of us kissed across his cock, his shaft like a log between the bridges of our mouths, a hard soft thing, that our tongues caressed over.

Samuel put his head back and smiled, satiated.

We helped each other back into our clothes, savouring final kisses. As Samuel clipped on my basque,

I rolled up Genevieve's stockings, tickling her inner thigh and laughing. She licked her tongue across the corners of my lips. I turned and planted a kiss on Samuel as he pulled on his shirt.

It was this moment I wanted to last the longest, actually. This feeling of oneness. Of experience shared. Of madness lived. Of not wanting to break the ring of lust that was formed in this spot, on this floor, in this house.

But soon, we could hear the cars pulling up outside and we knew that the spell had to be broken. We slunk downstairs, smiling at others who dragged themselves towards the door. I hoped that Samuel would come back with us. But he smiled graciously and said goodnight, stepping into a car with a nod of his head.

We drove off in the darkness, the two of us in the back seat, exhausted. Genevieve's fingers crept over the armrests until they were linked with mine. I smiled through my closed eyes.

'Thank you,' she whispered in the darkness.

I rolled my head towards her and peeked out from behind my eyelids.

Genevieve was weeping softly.

I immediately sat up and put my arm around her cradling her in my lap.

'What's the matter?' I asked.

'I hope I didn't ruin it,' she whispered.

'Ruin what?' I asked.

'You and Samuel,' she said. 'Me and Samuel.' And then she closed her eyes.

'You and me . . .'

'You didn't ruin anything,' I replied, her heart beating softly against my skin.

And then she said again, 'Thank you.'

I had no idea what she was talking about.

'Thank me for what?' I said, my lips touching her ear.

'Everything.'

I placed my hand on her cheek. I leaned over her, letting my hair block out the light from the road, so it was just the two of us, cradled in the back, two faces connected together. I kissed her on both her eyelids.

'I . . . *loved* it . . .' I whispered.

Genevieve turned her eyes towards me, and kissed me once on the lips.

The car pulled up the drive and we stepped out into the cool dawning air.

CHAPTER NINE

I woke up in Genevieve's bed. My head was deep in the crook of her neck and my arms wound their way behind her and around her, my hands clasped together beneath her breasts. We were both in T-shirts.

I opened my eyes and smelled her hair, the tangled golden mess that fell about my face. It smelled like Genevieve. Wild. Soft. Innocent. Natural. Untamed.

I kissed the back of her head and she groaned softly. Rolling on to my back I looked up at the ceiling and contemplated my future.

I was leaving today. That much I knew. Did I want to leave? Not really. Aside from wanting to stay in this bubble with Genevieve and the sun and the tingle, I knew the real world was calling me back. My main concern was that all the lessons I'd learned, all the freedom I had experienced, would fall away from me as soon as my feet touched the asphalt ground of the city.

Genevieve rolled over and stared up through her hair.

'Don't go . . .' she said.

'I think I have to,' I said, and she hugged me and I found myself feeling so wonderful to have this woman in my life, no matter how far apart we were. To have a sister. She was part of my life. Part of me. And I was proud of that.

I showered and changed and Genevieve and I joked over each other's clothes, and swapped things, and she went downstairs to make me a 'lavish' breakfast.

The breakfast was ridiculously abundant, brimming over with sausages, eggs, fresh fruit and even pancakes. We ate and laughed and stood in the garden.

After we had settled I told her there was something I wanted to do alone. She didn't ask me, she just smiled and said, 'I've got lots to get on with, anyway. I'll see you in a bit.'

I took the walk again. Over the changing-coloured fields. Past the whinnying horses padding by the wheat. Over to the fence. Through the bars and over to the stable.

It was colder now, and grey outside. I hugged myself as I edged to the door of the stable. Samuel was there, hanging saddles, polishing them. As was his way, he didn't turn to see me. He just knew I was there.

He continued to scrub at the saddle with the brush. 'You're leaving then?' he asked.

'In a few hours,' I answered.

I watched him work. Finally he seemed satisfied. He put down the brush and stepped towards me. He took my elbows in both his hands.

'You coming back?' he asked.

'One day,' I smiled.

'Well . . .' He trailed off.

He manoeuvred me round and eased me out of the stable by my shoulders. He looked ahead at the horses, at the horizon, at the sun. 'I have to go to London sometimes,' he murmured.

'Oh, really,' I replied.

'Yeah. Maybe I'll give you a call.'

'Maybe you should.' I smiled and turned to face him.

He took my face in both his hands. I could smell the sting of polish on his skin, mixed with his natural manly odour. I inhaled it for the last time, and let him kiss me, deep, full and passionate. I savoured the feel of his stubble, the scratch against my skin, the contrast of his soft, thick tongue. I savoured it all and then turned away from him.

And, as I walked back towards Genevieve's place, I didn't look back once.

Genevieve drove me to the station. When we got there we held each other tight and in silence.

'It's just been . . . thank you,' I mumbled.

'Thank *you*,' she said. 'My best student.'

And then we kissed, in full view of the old couple sitting nearby on the metal bench. I didn't care. Let them watch. Let them wonder.

The train pulled off through the green.

And I write this as the fields are being replaced by building works and roads. I am determined to be different. To be free. I will keep it up. Even if the grey outside world doesn't invite it.

My phone buzzes. It is a voicemail from Henry. He wants to meet up with me next week.

Well. Let him. I am strong enough to see him now. Open enough. Ready for him. Ready for anything . . .

EPILOGUE

FRIDAY 3RD JULY

Nearly three weeks have passed since I got back from the country. Work is fine. No, better than fine, it's good. I'm enjoying the new department. I am used to living alone now. It is OK. I see friends for dinner, I'm not in much, but I think I've learned to enjoy my 'alone' time now.

I have not been touched or caressed or held since my time in the country. I have taken long baths and discovered the pleasures of the shower head. But I have not found myself in any crazy situations at all. And I have longed for it.

Henry and I have had little contact. He moved in with Matt and I guess things are not great there. He has been calling fairly persistently. He sent me an email yesterday.

It made me cry. It said how much he missed me, how much he felt like he had ruined the best thing in his life. How he wanted me to understand that although he had fucked things up by being unfaithful, he couldn't believe he could ever jeopardize something as special as he had had emotionally with me. He finished by saying, 'And I can learn anything you want me to learn . . .'

I am seeing him tonight. I haven't seen him since I went away. I have always made sure to be out of the house when he comes to collect things.

For some reason I have tidied up. And lit some candles. And showered and dressed. And put on my nicest silk dress. Added thick black mascara to my eyelashes. For some reason my heart has been beating faster all day. Like I've been experiencing adrenaline.

Like I've had something to prove.

Which, of course, I do.

LATER

I met him at the back of Ladida on the King's Road. I picked that place because it had a nice area at the back, dimly lit with candles. And because it was not a place we had been together as a couple. It was neutral territory.

He was already there, also dressed smartly. He was wearing the shirt of his that he knew was my favourite. I liked the way it made him look like a businessman. The way it made him look older.

He stood up to greet me and we smiled at each other. The smile was genuine, I think, from both of us, and I let him kiss me half on the cheek and half on the lips. It felt odd to be in his thin arms. Odd because it was so familiar. I guess my body has memory of those arms. Many memories.

We sat down and he asked me questions about work and about friends. We drank some red wine and we laughed through the awkwardness by drawing attention to it. Which was what we had always done. Made jokes when things went bad. And it felt really good to do that here.

By the time we had finished the first bottle, the bar was getting busier, and Henry took the opportunity to move to the sofa next to me, so we weren't 'stealing a whole table . . .' As he sat down, our thighs faced forward, touching each other on the sides.

I smiled and we both went quiet, staring ahead, as a growing sense of sexual anticipation began to shiver over our skin, like an approaching army of little spiders.

I shook my head and tried to start the conversation again. Henry turned to me.

'Just listen to me . . .' His little finger brushed my thigh and I tingled. It had been a few weeks, and the thought of him touching me . . . well, it had its appeal.

He whispered urgently to me, with fervour, with meaning.

'We've had our time apart,' he said. 'I've missed you. Can't think of anything else. And I've thought about what I said to you that night. About how you're not open enough. And I'm sorry I said that. Because it was as much my problem as yours. I should have tried harder to explore things with you. I should have tried to share everything with you. I believe you could . . . I believe I could make you happy again.'

I listened to his words. He was right, of course. It takes two to tango, he could have tried harder, and I hadn't really known what I was missing, but still the memory of that moment in our room, catching him smearing chocolate over another woman, still prickled deep within me.

He put his hand on my arm, took it softly in his palm, and tried to turn me towards him. 'I believe I can try with you. If only you'll let me . . .'

He moved his lips towards me, tried to come in for a kiss. I changed position a little, letting it fall on to my neck. I whispered into his ear, 'Come back to the house.'

He blushed, then scrabbled for his coat. I walked ahead of him, my head held high. So he was coming back. To see if I was open. Well . . . let's see.

I unlocked the door. Henry seemed nervous, excited, his legs were trembling slightly. I opened up and we walked into the old place.

'You've changed it around,' he said, moving for the sofa.

'I thought it was a good idea.'

I moved over to the hi-fi and put on a Hotel Costes CD. Henry smiled as it played out of the speakers.

'Is it all right if I ...' he asked, motioning towards his shoes.

'Make yourself comfortable,' I replied.

I went into the kitchen and uncorked some more wine, poured the glasses and came back in. Henry had lit some of the candles and was sitting with his feet crossed in front of him and his hands on his lap. I came and sat next to him.

We clinked glasses and smiled. Henry sipped his, then put it down on the coffee table. He reached for my glass, took it from my hand and placed it next to his. He took my hands and looked into my eyes. 'I've wanted this for so long . . .'

He leaned forward, his lips slightly apart, and I let them kiss me, let that old familiar snugness take place. He pushed his tongue past my teeth, probing my mouth and breathing excitedly through his nose. He climbed on to me, forcing me back towards the sofa, his body on top of mine. I resisted as he put his weight on me, but he ignored me, scrabbling to undo his shirt and grab for my bottom.

I pushed him off me with both hands, and he fell against the sofa with a wounded look on his face. 'What's the matter?' he said, the candlelight giving him an even more innocent air.

I shook my head softly and bit my lip. I stood up in front of him, put a leg on each side of his legs. He looked up at me, bewildered. My fingers slipped inside each of the straps to my dress. I plucked at them, and with a soft woosh, the dress slipped past my breasts and fell to the floor.

My pussy, freshly cleaned and shaved and beautiful, was at his eye level. I put one leg on to the sofa, opened myself up, and Henry, with a face like a prisoner given parole, jumped forward, grabbing on to my bottom with both hands.

He buried his face into my stomach, kissing around it, and down, and then on to my thighs, and my calves, sticking my foot into his mouth, and then back up my calf, his tongue now sliding clean towards my pussy. He paused at the soft flesh of my inner thigh. He put his teeth around that flesh. And pressed down.

And what felt like a surge of electricity went round my body. I twisted my fingers into the roots of his hair and he groaned. I pulled his head in a circular motion, guiding his tongue inside and out. When he was dug deep inside me, I pushed down on him as hard as I could. I wanted him to discover the nub for himself, to feel it, to taste it, to understand what we had missed together.

He brought his tongue up to my clitoris, flicked it up and down in a frantic motion, pushing another finger inside me, which he pumped back and forth like he was in some kind of race. I took his hand away, and he looked up at me, his tongue pointing at my clitoris, and he smiled.

I placed his hand softly over my clitoris, and rotated it in a figure of eight. He began to lick the opening again, and I liked that, that was good, and he reached down and scrabbled at his belt.

Beneath me his cock stood up hard and proud, groping higher, wanting to make contact with its old friend. Henry held his cock at the base, and began to stroke it up and down, his other hand on my pussy.

I stepped down from the sofa, turned my bottom towards Henry's face, and then lowered myself into his lap. His cock went inside and I ground down on to it, trying to get it in deep, to feel the filling-up sensation that so overwhelms me.

Henry squeezed my breasts and began to thrust upward from his hips. My ankles strained below my calves as we half stood, half sat, Henry fucking me, his face buried in my hair. I rubbed myself with my right hand and with my left hand I reached behind me to pinch Henry's nipples.

Henry groaned and slapped my bottom, then squeezed it as it shook. He took hold of my hips and thrust hard into me, raising himself up and up, and suddenly he was close to the nub, he was going to find it, and I closed my eyes.

His cock grazed the nub, found it, flirted with it and retracted, but it was enough to set me off and I nodded, yes, that's it, yes, right there, don't stop, please, touch it, you're there, that's it, please . . .

Henry was overexcited. He was sweating and grunting and I knew he was close to exploding. I pressed down on him, grinding into his hips with more speed and force, and I could feel him try to hold me up, try to slow it down, he didn't want to come now, he wanted to slow down, he wanted to hold on, but I wouldn't let him. I pushed down and down and held his hand to my breast and covered his face with my hair, and pushed and pushed and screamed and let it all out.

He froze, his face torn in wretched concentration, and he thrust one more time, shooting his come deep inside me, deep into my pussy, trying for one last grope, the cum an extension of his cock, reaching into me.

He breathed so heavily it sounded as if he might be having some kind of attack, and I stayed on him, let him stay in me until his cock retreated and came out, slimy and satisfied. He put his arms up above him and said, 'That was . . . amazing . . . amazing.'

He smiled and tried to bring me towards him for another kiss. Instead I stood up and went into the bathroom. At the door I called to him, 'Let me know when you can go again,' and shut the door.

I ran a bath. Stood by it, the door locked. I stared at the steam and thought about what I was doing. What was I doing?

I sat on the toilet, let his sperm fall out into the bowl, and wiped myself down. There was more to this. I didn't just want sex. I wanted to show him something. That's what this was about. I wanted . . . reparation.

There was a knock at the door.

'What do you want?' I asked.

'I want to come in . . . I'm not quite ready, but in two minutes I will be.'

'Then come back in two minutes,' I said, and turned the heat up on the bath.

'What's your fantasy?' I called through the door.

'What?' he mumbled.

'If you could do anything to me. What would it be?'

There was a pause.

Henry was thinking.

'Anything at all?' he asked.

'It's a question, Henry. Answer it.'

'I guess it would be to have anal sex with you . . .'

I looked at the door. Henry was so predictable.

'How are you now?'

I knew the conversation would have got him excited. 'Yeah,' he called. 'I could go again. I like the new you.'

I heard that and it sat funny with me. 'The new me'. It was true I had experienced things. I had tried new and amazing sexual scenarios. I had found a sexual comfort within myself. All of this was true.

But I had found it all without Henry. The man I had been with for so many years. And yet it had needed me to leave him for me to find myself.

I turned off the taps, flicked the lock on the door and stepped into the water. The heat sent a shiver up my spine. I sat down in the bath and let the bubbles cover my skin.

Henry opened the door. He stood against the doorframe, his cock held half-erect in his hand. He smiled at me, sheepishly.

I narrowed my eyes and stared at him. 'So that's what you want? Anal sex?' I asked.

'Yes,' said Henry. 'Or to make love to you and another woman ... or watch you with another woman ...'

His cock grew harder as he talked and I watched it grow, sliding my hands over my breasts and back between my legs. 'Tell me about that,' I said, and Henry came further into the bathroom, gently stroking his penis in front of him.

He took a seat on the towel basket and leaned back against the wall, his eyes on my soapy breasts. 'I guess you'd be alone. In the bath. And I'd come in. And you would be playing with yourself . . .'

I began to slide my hand through the folds of myself.

'Then you'd gasp a little as the door opened. You weren't expecting me. And then, overexcited, you turn over in the bath . . .'

I looked at him and breathed out slowly through my mouth.

OK.

I turned over on to my hands and knees. The bubbly water sloshed between my legs.

'And I would bend down towards your arse . . .'

He stood up and walked towards the bath. And then he crouched down.

'And I would put my mouth over your arse.' He did this. 'Then slip my tongue right inside you.' I felt his tongue trip over knots of nerves and I shuddered involuntarily. 'And then I would hold you around the waist, running my tongue over your pussy, and all the way over your arse, then back to your pussy, until you couldn't take it any more . . .'

I shut my eyes, and let his tongue do exactly what he had promised. It was a new feeling, a kind of nervous tingling that spread from the inside out. I kept my eyes closed and enjoyed it for the moment that I could.

For I had already let this go too far. I had a plan and I needed to stick to it. To not get carried away by all this.

His tongue probed deep inside my asshole and I flinched as it did. He spoke again, his lips on my buttocks. 'And then I kiss you all over, and you ask me to fuck you, you ask me to go inside you, you tell me to do it . . .'

I spoke. 'Now you have to go.'

'What?' said Henry, a small laugh escaping his lips. I pulled away from him and turned over. I stood up, the bubbles dripping down my oily skin.

'Are you joking?' he asked, his hands on my thighs, his cock bursting between his legs.

I looked down at him. 'You could have had all this,' I said. 'It was all yours. All you had to do was communicate with me. To show me. To help me. To include me. That's all you had to do . . .'

And Henry kissed my thighs and whispered, 'Oh God, of course, I understand that, I completely understand that, and that's why I'm going to make things right . . .'

I pushed him off my thighs and looked into his eyes. I crouched down so that my lips could be at his ear.

'You missed your chance.'

And with that I stepped out of the bath, wrapping a warm towel around me. I stepped out into the living room, leaving Henry staggering about and protesting in the bathroom.

Finally, Henry left, his face burning, his hands fumbling for one last kiss, but I closed the door on him and took a deep breath.

I was free. Restored. Taken care of.

I moved back to the bathroom. The water was still hot. I saw no reason not to get back in.

After all, I had next week to think about.

When a certain stableboy was coming to town to pay me a visit. I pushed my fingers inside myself. It felt nice to be warm and familiar and in good hands. I looked at my nipples, peeking out over the surface of the water and I had a thought.

I must give Genevieve a call tomorrow . . . she should come and stay too.